AN ORIGINAL NOVEL

UNDERTOW

AN ORIGINAL NOVEL

BY STEVE BEHLING

AQUAMAN CREATED BY
PAUL NORRIS AND MORT WEISINGER

HARPER

An Imprint of HarperCollinsPublishers

Aquaman: Undertow
Copyright © 2018 DC Comics and Warner Bros. Entertainment Inc.
AQUAMAN and all related characters and elements © & ™
DC Comics and Warner Bros. Entertainment Inc.
(s18)
HARP41451

ISBN 978-0-06-287419-1
Library of Congress Control Number: 2018952747
Typography by Erica De Chavez
18 19 20 21 22 PC/LSCH   10 9 8 7 6 5 4 3 2 1
❖
First Edition

To my mom and dad,
who encouraged me to read comics.

And to Ramona Fradon, whose art and
storytelling made Aquaman come alive.

PROLOGUE

"YOU KNOW WHAT YOUR PROBLEM is? You just sit there, waiting for life to happen. You have to go out and *make* it happen. Pretty wise words, right?"

The water was warm for this time of year, but it barely registered with Arthur Curry as he dipped a foot into the ocean. He was too deep in conversation to really care about the temperature of the water. Not that he ever really cared about things like that, anyway.

To a person who could survive the crushing pressures of the deepest parts of the world's oceans, a little thing like warm or cold water was exactly that—little.

"I know what you're going to say. 'Well, what have *you* done?' That's a fair question. But I have done a lot. So much. I've gotten so much done. Even this morning, before breakfast."

Arthur looked down at the dock as he sat, his legs dangling over the side. Staring into the water, his eyes met another set of eyes, breaking just above the ocean's surface.

"Don't look at me like that," Arthur said, dismissing the eyes in the water with a wave of his hand. "Are you giving *me* side eye? Really?" He looked behind him and saw the lighthouse. He had called it home for as long as he could remember.

Until the day he left.

"Okay, so it's gonna be like that, huh?" Arthur huffed. "Well, I've saved the world, for starters. That's pretty good, right? That's doing something. Have you saved the world? Have you?"

Arthur paused for a moment, as if awaiting a response that would never come.

"Yeah, that's what I thought."

His attention turned back to the lighthouse, and the memories of childhood flooded his mind. Happy memories, for the most part. But there was always a cloud hanging over even the happiest of those memories. He loved his father to the ends of the earth and back, from its highest peak to its greatest depths, deep down in the ocean. The ocean . . .

"Why am I telling you all this? Killing time. Don't get me wrong, it's good to see you, but I'm waiting for my dad."

Tom Curry, the lighthouse keeper. Ever since Arthur could remember, that was Tom's job: to keep the shores free of shipwrecks. He had to maintain the beacon and make sure it was in working order every day. More and more lighthouses were automated these days, but the Amnesty Bay lighthouse still required a human operator. It was a job he took seriously, but he himself was not a serious man. Tom had a sense of humor, one which he instilled in his son. Humor was a key commodity in the Curry household.

Sometimes, laughter was all they had. It was that sense of humor that had helped Arthur through some pretty tough moments in his childhood.

"He should be here any minute," Arthur said, looking into the water as the eyes bobbed up and down. "I know, I know. It's weird that I'm the one who showed up early."

He stood, picked up a piece of driftwood from the dock, and raised it in the air.

"Go get the stick! Go! Fetch!"

Then he hurled the driftwood right over the octopus's head. It sailed for maybe a hundred feet, then landed in the ocean with a distant *plop*.

The octopus didn't budge. It didn't blink. It didn't do anything.

"We gotta work on that, buddy," Arthur said.

He stood up and felt the warm sun beating down upon his tattooed torso and arms. Then he scratched his beard and stared at the octopus, which was now sitting on a rock in the water.

"Anyway, good talk, Topo," Arthur said, waving at the octopus.

CHAPTER
ONE

THE MEMORY WAS WITHOUT

color, just shades of black and gray and pure, shimmering white.

It began as it always did. There was the sun. A great arc of white, it had just started to peek out from the horizon. There was a chill in the air, and even though he was bundled up, he was cold.

He remembered that much.

They say you don't start forming memories until you're three years old. Or, at least, you can't remember anything that happened *before* you were three. That's how it was with Arthur Curry. The earliest memory of his mother—his only memory of her, really—came from when he was three years old.

He was on a dock.

The dock.

Then there was the woman. Her hair was long, and he could see her face. But the features remained elusive, like clay that had yet to be sculpted. The expression was there—that much he could see. She was smiling at him. There was kindness in the smile; he could feel that. But he could feel something else, too.

Sadness?

Yes, sadness. For there was crying, too. Mournful crying, the sound of someone doing something they don't want to do but know they must.

But he wasn't the one crying, and they weren't his tears.

It was the woman. She was crying.

And the man standing next to her.

The man in the memory, Arthur knew very well. The face belonged to his father, Tom.

Arthur remembered the woman holding him tightly, their faces pressed close together. A trickle of tears ran from her cheek and onto Arthur's.

Words were spoken, by both the mysterious woman and his father. He couldn't remember what they said. They weren't talking to him, Arthur knew that much. He looked at them both, curious. They looked sad, and even the sound of their words evoked sorrow.

The ocean waves lapped the dock beneath his feet, the sea spraying up on the weather-worn wood. Even at a young age, he had been fascinated by the water. By the ocean. He could remember how it felt on his feet.

More tears.

More sorrowful words.

The woman, holding Arthur so tight he thought he might burst.

The man, plaintive.

And then, a kiss on his forehead, her lips

cool. A hand touched his cheek, gently brushing away a lock of hair.

Then the woman kissed his father. And she turned away from them, looking out toward the vast ocean before her. To his surprise, the woman didn't turn around to look at father or son.

She dived into the water, never to be seen again.

CHAPTER
TWO

"DID SHE LIKE FRENCH FRIES?"

The man laughed as he picked up a smooth stone from the sandy beach. "Yeah, she liked French fries."

"With ketchup?" Arthur asked. It was the kind of question a six-year-old would ask. This was important stuff, and Arthur wanted to file the information away for future reference.

The man, Tom Curry, looked at the rock in his right hand, grasped between his thumb and index finger. Then he drew the arm back, and whipped it forward, releasing the rock. The stone sailed through the air, very low, then hit the surface of the water, glancing off once, then twice, then three times, before it finally landed with a satisfying *plop* in the ocean.

"With ketchup," Tom said. "And mayonnaise."

"Mayonnaise?" Arthur gasped in legitimate horror. "That's gross! Why would she ruin French fries?"

Tom laughed again. "I don't think she was trying to ruin them, kid. She just liked them that way, is all."

Arthur thought about this for a minute and shrugged his shoulders as if to say, *I guess that's possible.* Then he picked up a rock. "I bet I can skip it more times than you," Arthur said to his father.

Tom nodded. "Maybe so. Let's see what you've got."

The boy held the stone just like his father had shown him. Then he started to walk toward the water, and then he started to run, the sand beneath his feet going from grainy and dry to wet and clumpy.

"Arthur! You're in the water!"

But the boy wasn't listening, and before he knew it, his feet were in the shallows, water around his ankles. He released the rock from his right hand and watched hopefully as it hit the ocean surface once, then promptly sank. Dejected, he turned around, looking at his rock-throwing mentor.

"You'll get the hang of it, kid," Tom said, walking toward his son. "And next time, don't run into the water. Just stay on the sand, like I did."

"Okay, Dad," Arthur replied. He stomped his feet in the wet sand, trying in vain to hide his disappointment at not being able to skip rocks just like his dad. The water flowed all around his ankles. Something brushed against his left foot, and he thought it might have been seaweed, brought in by the tide.

Then it touched his right foot.

Then his left again.

"What's going on, kid?" Tom asked, noticing Arthur's distraction.

"Something keeps touching my feet," Arthur said, gazing into the murky water.

The touch came again, and this time he saw it—a tentacle. With suckers. Then he saw what the tentacle was attached to. An octopus.

A baby octopus. The creature poked its bulbous head through the water's surface, and Arthur let out a laugh.

Tom put his hand on Arthur's shoulder and chuckled. "Looks like you've found a friend," he said. "Lots of octopi in these waters, but I don't remember seeing one so close to shore before. Certainly not a . . . looks like a baby Pacific."

"Are they really pie?" Arthur said as the baby octopus stroked his foot with one of its tentacles.

"Are they what?" Tom said.

"You called them 'octo-pie.' Are they really pie?"

Tom laughed again. "You mean like dessert pie?" he said, shaking his head. "No, that's just what you call a bunch of octopuses. Octopi."

"But why not call 'em 'octopuses' like you just did?" Arthur asked.

The man let out a soft sigh, put his arm around Arthur, and they started to walk along the beach.

"Because people are strange and make up weird rules," Tom said.

"Like putting mayonnaise on French fries?" Arthur asked. Tom laughed and ruffled his son's hair.

Arthur took a bite of his peanut butter and jelly sandwich (no crusts, cut into triangles) as they sat on the dock, watching the fishing boats come in. "Yoo puhhhhh ahhh oooo muuuhhhh peeeenuhhh buhhhh!" Arthur said, his mouth full of sandwich.

"Pretend I could understand even a word of what you just said," Tom said, taking a bite of his own sandwich.

Taking a big swig of milk from the thermos, Arthur washed down the sandwich in his mouth. "I said, you put on too much peanut butter! I don't like it with that much peanut butter, only a little."

Tom straightened up and looked at the sandwich in his hands. "I guess there is a lot of peanut butter. I like it that way."

"Well, I don't," Arthur said. "Can you make it with less next time?"

"Of course," Tom said. "Your wish is my command."

The waves splashed the rocks in the distance, and Arthur thought he saw something.

A tentacle.

Was it . . . ? It was! It was the baby octopus. Perched on the rock. Like . . . like it was watching him.

"Can you tell me about Mom?" Arthur asked.

Tom took another bite. "What do you want to know?"

"Anything. Like, how did you and Mom meet?" Arthur looked at his dad, eyes open wide. It was a look that Tom was unable to resist, though he tried.

"That story? *Again?* Arthur, I've told it to you, like, a hundred times. A hundred times a hundred times."

Arthur hit his father on the shoulder playfully. "I know, but I like it! It's a good story!"

Tom finished chewing the bite of sandwich and relented. "Okay, okay. I know I'm not going to win this one. So, the day I first saw your mother, it—"

"'It was a dark and stormy night,'" Arthur interjected. "That's how the story starts."

Tom raised both hands, as if to surrender. "I stand corrected. It was a dark and stormy night, one of the darkest and stormiest nights that Amnesty Bay had ever seen.

I was outside, battening the hatches, securing the lighthouse against the storm, when what should I see?"

"Mom!" Arthur whooped.

"Well, yes, but she wasn't your mom yet. She was then a strange and mysterious woman, lying faceup in the water. She was hurt. And she was holding—"

"A TRIDENT!" Arthur yelled. He grabbed the thermos and raised it high over his head, like he was holding a trident, too, spilling a little milk in the process.

Tom laughed. "Yes, a trident. You know what a trident is, right?"

In unison, both father and son shouted, "SEA FORK!" and cracked up.

Arthur slapped his hand on his knee, then noticed something move in the distance. It was the octopus. Arthur slapped his knee again, and then he saw the octopus slap the water with a tentacle, almost as if in response.

Instinctively, Arthur waved.

CHAPTER
THREE

IT WAS COLD INSIDE THE CURRYS' house. Arthur was wearing an oversized, bulky knit sweater that threatened to devour him. He liked the orange-and-green sweater. His father told him that his mother used to wear it. Arthur swore that he could smell his mom whenever he wore it. But truthfully, he couldn't remember what she smelled like.

"With meatballs or without?"

Arthur walked into the kitchen, and saw his father holding a can of premade pasta in each hand. Spaghetti in one, spaghetti and meatballs in the other. Thinking for a moment, Arthur pointed at Tom's right hand. "With!" he shouted.

"Meatballs it is," Tom said, opening a drawer and reaching for the can opener.

"Can I help?" Arthur asked.

"Yeah, sure," Tom replied. As he cranked the can opener, he gestured with his chin toward a nearby cabinet. "Can you get the pot?"

The young boy ran to the cabinet, his socks skidding along the smooth tile of the kitchen floor. Tom started to laugh. "Why walk when you can run? Why run when you can slide?"

The words didn't register with Arthur, who was already at the cabinet. Throwing the door open, Arthur dug around inside, and the sound of clanging pans echoed in the tiny kitchen. Tom winced with each new *clang*, but Arthur was undeterred. A few seconds later, the boy emerged from the cabinet holding a blue saucepan, its paint chipped and worn away in places. He held it in his right hand, raised over his head, like a sword.

"Mission accomplished!" Arthur announced, and Tom had to laugh again.

"Set it on the stove, kid," Tom said, and Arthur placed the saucepan on a front burner.

Arthur watched as his father poured the contents of the can into the pan and turned on the gas burner. There was a *click*, the smell of gas, a spark, and then a flame. Tom grabbed a big spoon from a container on the counter and handed it to Arthur. "You stir, like I showed you," he said.

Arthur grasped the large wooden spoon in his hand and stirred the pasta awkwardly.

"You're turning into a real chef," Tom said. "Your mom would be proud."

Arthur smiled, but the grin quickly turned to a frown, and he stopped stirring. "Where is Mom?" he said, without looking up. The tone was impatient.

Tom shifted on his feet uncomfortably. "She's out there, somewhere," Tom said, pointing an index finger out the kitchen window, at the ocean beyond.

"You always say that," Arthur said, a note of irritation in his voice.

"That's because it's true," Tom said, as he gently ran a hand along Arthur's back. "When I—when we said goodbye to your mother, she was on the dock, and she jumped into the ocean. And as far as I know, that's where she still is."

"Then why doesn't she come back?" Arthur asked, banging the spoon against the sides of the pan. "What is she waiting for?"

Tom placed his large, weathered hand over his son's, and gently stopped the spoon from banging the sides, then slowly started stirring again. "Only she knows" was his reply. "And we have to trust her."

The boy looked up at his father, eyes piercing. "Where is she?"

The voice wasn't asking. It was demanding.

Tom looked at his son and bit his lower lip. Then he turned off the burner on the stove and moved the pan of spaghetti and meatballs off the heat. He put the pan on the small table, on top of a pot holder. Then he went to a drawer, grabbed two forks, and offered one to Arthur.

"Sit down, dinner's ready."

Arthur grabbed the fork, then sat down. "I'm not hungry," he said, letting his fork drop to the table.

Swirling his fork in the pan, Tom collected strands of spaghetti, then stabbed a meatball. He shoved the food into his mouth, then looked at Arthur. The boy just sat there staring, his eyes big and unblinking.

"There were . . . some people who were after your mother," Tom said, and Arthur instantly perked up.

"What people?" Arthur asked. "Why did they want Mom? Can we go after them?"

Tom shook his head no, chewing his food. "That would defeat the purpose of her leaving in the first place."

"I don't get it," Arthur said, confused.

"She left because . . . because she was in trouble," Tom said. "And she didn't want you and me . . . especially you . . . to be in trouble, too." He pushed the fork toward Arthur, who picked it up in his right hand. The boy stuck the fork into the pan and swirled some pasta. "Glad to see you got your appetite back."

"We should help her."

Tom thought for a second. "I wish we could, kid," Tom said. "But it's more complicated than that. I . . . I'm not explaining it very well, am I?"

The two sat in silence for a moment as they continued to eat their dinner from the same pan. Arthur rubbed his nose, then looked at his father. "Why couldn't she bring us with her?"

"Sometimes . . . sometimes people go places where we can't follow, Arthur," Tom said.

"Are you gonna go?"

Tom looked at his son and shook his head. "You're stuck with me," he said.

He couldn't breathe.

Struggling to take in a breath, Arthur found that no matter how hard he tried, he couldn't inhale. It was like the air was a solid, or a liquid.

A liquid?

Water.

The ocean.

He was in the ocean, but it wasn't blue or green. It was dark. Very dark. And Arthur knew that he was deep below the ocean's surface. His hands, arms, and legs were in motion, as if treading water to keep in place. But it required almost no effort. Arthur felt as if his limbs were unencumbered, as if there was no resistance.

It was impossible to tell how long he had been there, treading water, or how he got there. Peering through the darkness, Arthur could see small fish swimming his way, then suddenly scattering. He looked around and saw a long, dark shape coming closer. It was the size of a person, maybe larger.

As it grew closer, Arthur saw that the shape had eyes.

And teeth.

Shark.

He felt something brush against his back, and he whirled around in the water. His eyes caught a glimpse of a tail and another shark.

Then another.

And another.

They were circling him now, the sharks.

Arthur felt his pulse throbbing in his temples, his throat seizing up.

And still the sharks circled.

What were they waiting for? Why didn't they attack?

Spinning around, Arthur watched as the sharks swam, keeping their distance. They were close but didn't seem interested in him, Arthur realized. It was almost like they were there to . . . protect him? Growing bold, Arthur decided to swim toward one of the sharks. With the pull of his right arm, he tried to swim ahead, only to find the sharks

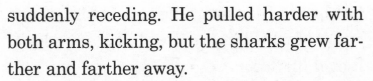

suddenly receding. He pulled harder with both arms, kicking, but the sharks grew farther and farther away.

And he screamed, but no sound came out.

"Hey, hey, I'm here, I'm here!"

Arthur felt himself shaking, only he wasn't the one doing it. It was his father, hair looking crazy, bleary-eyed. The boy looked around his bedroom and saw the alarm clock—2:13 a.m. His father's hands were on either shoulder, now holding Arthur steady.

"You got a set of lungs on you, kid," Tom said. "You started screaming, and I came running. Must have been some dream."

"I was screaming?" Arthur said, as if he hadn't heard anything his father had said.

"You were screaming."

"I . . . had a weird dream."

"How about you tell me all about it after we both get some more sleep?" Tom said, standing up. He grabbed the blanket that had been balled up at the bottom of Arthur's bed, unfurled it, gave it a shake, and placed it over his son.

"Yeah, okay," Arthur said.

"G'night, Arthur."

"G'night, Dad," Arthur replied, and watched as his father disappeared behind the closed door.

CHAPTER
FOUR

"OKAY, CLASS, LET'S HEAR IT ONE
more time."

"No talking."

"No touching."

"No shoving."

"No having fun."

Mrs. Lewis craned her neck, looking down
the aisle of the bus and over the heads of her
fourth-grade class, trying to see who'd lobbed
in that last comment. Her eyes drifted to a
seat occupied by two of the taller boys in
the group, Matt and Mike. They both barely

stifled their laughs, easily heard among the murmuring students.

With a sigh, Mrs. Lewis continued, "Field trips are a privilege, not a right. If you act like buffoons, I will treat you like buffoons, and we'll stay on the bus and head back to Amnesty Bay." The bus fell silent, with Matt and Mike attempting to wipe the smiles from their faces and failing miserably.

Arthur looked out the window of the bus at the Boston Aquarium. Ever since he could remember, he'd loved visiting the place. There was something about all the sea creatures that fired Arthur's imagination. He could stare at them for hours, watching them, wondering what their lives must be like. His father would bring him there at least two or three times a year, sometimes more, if Arthur begged enough.

He usually begged enough.

"All right, then. Now that we understand each other, let's get off the bus and assemble by the entrance. Remember: stick with your *assigned* partners."

The students stood up from their seats and, front to back, began to file out of the bus. Arthur, sitting in the back, watched everyone leave until it was his turn to stand and exit. As he shuffled along the aisle, waiting to depart, he looked out the windows and saw the other students pairing up. Mrs. Lewis had assigned each student a field-trip partner, and Arthur was unhappily surprised to find out that he was stuck with Matt. In addition to being a self-styled "class clown," Matt was also a straight-up bully. And he liked to direct all that bullying toward Arthur.

The last one off the bus, Arthur hit the parking lot, and saw that Matt had already paired off with his fellow bully Mike.

"Hey, we're supposed to be field-trip partners," Arthur said, halfheartedly.

"Yeah? Well, I already got a partner," Matt said, and he gave Arthur a little shove to emphasize his point. "Who knows? Maybe you'll find your mom inside, fish boy." Then he laughed and walked away with Mike.

"You can stick with us, Arthur," said Mrs. Lewis, who was standing with another student, Claudia. She was a little taller than Arthur, with brown hair and round, freckled cheeks, and one of her front permanent teeth had yet to come in. The teacher shook her head and muttered, "Matt and Mike deserve each other."

"All life came from the seas," the tour guide announced, "so if we want to understand ourselves, we must journey to where we began."

The guide gestured to the enormous glass wall behind them, which contained the tropical coral reef exhibit. It was stunning, and Arthur was transfixed. The coral was teeming with life. Fish of all shapes and sizes darted in and out, their vibrant colors a blur.

Arthur saw stingrays and eels swimming along, following no discernible path.

"The tank you see behind me holds approximately two hundred thousand gallons of salt water, simulating an ocean environment. The various fish in this tank can all be found in the Caribbean, and the Boston Aquarium has spared no expense to make them feel at home right here," the tour guide said, waving her hand along the glass, showing off the tank.

Arthur stood, feet planted, looking through the glass at the mass of life that thrived beyond. He saw a moray eel and tried to predict the path it would follow. Impossible. The eel wriggled, its body rippling. A shark swam past and caught Arthur's eye. He shuddered. He'd had dreams about sharks. Had ever since he was six. Arthur didn't know why, but he did.

"What'cha lookin' at, freak?"

The next thing Arthur knew, a hand was

palming the back of his head, and his face was shoved against the glass tank. Arthur winced.

"Fish boy's checking out his only friends, the fishes!" Matt said, laughing.

"I'm not a fish boy!" Arthur snapped. Matt always called him "fish boy," and he hated it. Arthur couldn't decide if Matt was doing it just because he thought he was being funny, or if he really did think that Arthur was part fish. Matt wasn't exactly the brightest fly in the tackle box.

"Oh yeah?" Mike added. "Then where's your mom, fish boy?"

"Leave me alone!" Arthur said, his lips mushed against the glass.

"Yeah, leave him alone!"

The voice came from behind Matt, and Arthur saw Claudia standing there, her right hand balled up in a fist. "Let him go, jerk!" Claudia said.

"What, is fish boy your boyfriend now?" Matt said, his hand still pressed against the back of Arthur's head.

"I'm gonna give you five seconds to let go of him, and then I'm gonna get mad," Claudia said, and everything in her voice said she was serious.

"Claudia, why don't you go join the rest of the class," said a stern voice. "And Matt, Mike—why *don't* you leave Arthur alone," Mrs. Lewis interjected, jabbing a finger in Matt's chest. The bully let go of Arthur. Mrs. Lewis put a strong hand on the backs of both Matt and Mike and guided them away from Arthur. "I'll be talking to your parents," she said. "And coming up with some incredibly difficult homework assignments for you both."

Arthur took a deep breath. Why did Claudia do that? Matt and Mike were such bullies. Why would she make herself a target, too?

He didn't have an answer. And he wasn't used to someone having his back at school. It felt . . . good.

Turning back to the tank, Arthur watched as the fish swam behind the glass. *They seem curious about the human looking at them*, Arthur thought. *Maybe they're just as curious about me as I am about them?*

The sound of laughter interrupted Arthur's thoughts, and he turned to see the rest of his classmates cracking up as Matt and Mike made goofy faces at the fish in the tank, and knocking on the glass.

"Today we have better maps of Mars than we do of our own seafloor," the tour guide said, then noticed Matt and Mike. "Boys, stop that. Come along . . ."

The rest of the class moved away, following the guide, with Mrs. Lewis and Claudia right behind.

Swiveling his head from the class to the tank, Arthur was stunned to see a large sea turtle staring right back at him, its head only inches away.

"Whoa!" Arthur said out loud. He leaned in to get a better look. To his surprise, the sea turtle did the exact same thing. It was almost as if the creature was mimicking

Arthur. "This is unreal," Arthur said in a voice just above a whisper.

The staring contest continued for at least a minute before Arthur became aware that they had company. Other sea life in the tank had joined the sea turtle. Now a small school of rainbow fish were staring at Arthur, and he, back at them. If he swayed left, they swayed left. If he swayed right, they, too, swayed right.

No way . . .

As Arthur watched, the sounds of the aquarium seemed to fade away to nothingness. In their place, there was a low thrumming sensation in his head. It wasn't a sound, and it wasn't mechanical, it was . . . it was something else. Like a feeling. Organic. Alive. Was it his imagination, or was it . . . coming from the tank?

At once, the thrumming sensation in his head stopped, as Arthur found himself thrown up against the glass.

"Let me go!" Arthur shouted, Matt grabbing his shirt and banging him up against

the glass. Arthur noticed that the crowd of classmates and other aquarium visitors were now staring at him.

"You're such a freak, Arthur!" Matt sneered.

His back was pressed against the glass as Arthur watched Matt and Mike continue their taunting, their name calling, their bullying. Their words were painful and hurt Arthur. But mostly, they made him angry. He felt something inside him begin to boil. His fists clenched, the thrumming sensation in his head started again, the strange feeling that he had earlier returning. He saw Matt's eyes go wide. Mike's eyes went wide, too. Arthur wondered what was going on. Then he heard it.

WHAM!

Arthur felt the impact, and the vibration running along and down his back. He whirled around, only to see a shark . . . all ten feet of it, its head floating right next to the glass, its black, unblinking eyes staring right at Matt.

"What the . . . ," Matt muttered.

The crowd let out an audible gasp as the shark circled around, building up momentum, and struck the glass again in the exact point it had hit before.

WHAM!

The creature hit the glass wall of the tank with such force that a crack at the point of impact began to spider across the entire container. Then another crack. Then another. They, too, began to spider in various directions.

And water began to trickle out from the cracks.

"What's going—"

Arthur turned to see the tour guide running back, a look of shock on her face as she saw the damaged glass.

"Get back!" the tour guide shouted. Mrs. Lewis was right behind her, her mouth wide open, horrified.

"Arthur!" she called. "Are you all right?"

The tour guide stood slack-jawed, not

knowing what to do. A crowd had now assembled around the tank, and no one seemed to know what to do as the shark circled around, and started for the glass once more. A hush fell over the room as everyone waited for the inevitable, half expecting a rush of water and a hungry shark to come spilling into the aquarium itself.

Then, just before the shark could strike, Arthur held up a hand as if telling the shark to . . . stop. Was it instinct? Was it something else?

Whatever it was, to his and everyone else's shock, the shark stopped before it could strike the glass again. And like the sea turtle before, the shark now hovered in the water, looking into Arthur's eyes, Arthur looking back.

Once again, Arthur felt the strange thrumming sensation, a feeling he just couldn't place. The feeling grew stronger and stronger, as Arthur realized that they were not alone. The shark had been joined by an

incredible assortment of tropical fish, octopi, mantas, and eels. They were all facing forward, looking at Arthur.

Arthur felt someone grasp his arm, and turned to see Claudia, looking at him in wonder. "You . . . you calmed them down," Claudia said in awe.

CHAPTER
FIVE

WHAT A WEIRD DAY.

The rest of the field trip was a blur for everyone. All they could talk about was the "shark attack" at the aquarium, with students swearing up and down that the shark was THIS CLOSE to escaping, and how it would have eaten everyone. On the bus ride back to school, it was like a game of telephone, as kids in one seat would relate some aspect of the day's events to the kids behind them, and then those kids would add something as they told their version of the story to the students behind them.

Arthur sat on the bus, next to Claudia. He didn't say a word, and she didn't, either. But he felt like everyone on the bus was staring at him.

Maybe I am some kind of freak . . . some kind of . . . fish boy, he thought.

And the whole way back to school, Matt and Mike sat next to Mrs. Lewis, as she laid out the incredible amount of homework the two would be doing from now until sometime in the next century.

When they got to the front of the school, Arthur waited until Matt and Mike got off the bus, and their not-too-happy parents picked them up.

"Are you gonna leave sometime today?" the bus driver asked Arthur. Then he walked down the aisle and stepped out into the school parking lot.

"Your dad coming?" Mrs. Lewis asked.

Arthur shook his head. "Working in the lighthouse today."

"An important job," Mrs. Lewis said, trying to shore up Arthur's spirits. "You'll be okay walking home?"

"Yeah," Arthur replied. "Thanks for the field trip, Mrs. Lewis."

"You're welcome. Get home safe," Mrs. Lewis said, as Arthur walked through the parking lot and down the street in front of the school.

Arthur kicked a rock to see how far it would go. Launched from the toe of his left sneaker, the rock hit the Myerses' mailbox, ricocheted off, and missed their front window by an inch. Arthur winced just thinking what would have happened if it HAD hit their window.

"Nice shot."

Whirling around, Arthur saw Claudia, her book bag slung over her right shoulder, a strap dangling behind her, dragging on the ground.

"Uh, hey," Arthur said shyly.

"Can I walk with you?" Claudia asked, but

she wasn't really asking. She had already caught up to Arthur, matching his stride. "Were you trying to break that window?"

"No," Arthur said, defiant. "It was just an accident. I kicked—"

"Relax, I'm kidding," Claudia said. "Y'know, sometimes I watch you and . . . and you're so *serious*."

"I guess nothing's very funny," Arthur answered.

"Like Matt and Mike?"

There was a brief pause. "I don't wanna talk about it," Arthur said. "Whatever. It's over and done with."

Claudia shrugged her shoulders as they walked along the side of the rock-strewn road. "Then what do you wanna talk about? Like how about all those fish at the aquarium? That was freaky, right?"

"Yeah." Arthur nodded. "Freaky."

"All those fish, just looking at you . . . You're like the fish whisperer or something," Claudia said, laughing at her own joke. When Arthur didn't join in, she stopped. "Are you—all right?"

"I'm fine, okay?" Arthur said, his temper beginning to flare. "I just don't want to talk about it! I just wanna be left alone!"

Arthur walked ahead by himself.

A few seconds later, he had the weird feeling that someone was right behind him.

"You could say 'you're welcome,' y'know," Claudia muttered.

"What?" Arthur said, kicking a rock. He turned around and looked at Claudia, who stared at him briefly before looking away, shaking her head. Then he realized what she was talking about.

The aquarium. Matt and Mike. Arthur closed his eyes and sighed.

"I'm sorry," Arthur said. "Thanks."

"You're welcome," Claudia said. "I would have done it, y'know." She made a fist with her right hand, then crashed it into her open left palm. Then she wiggled the fingers on her left hand and moved them away, making an explosion sound.

At that, Arthur let out a small laugh. "Yeah, I believe you woulda hit Matt."

"And he woulda gone down, too," Claudia said.

"How'd you get so tough?" Arthur asked.

"Two brothers," she replied. "One older, one younger. Both pains in the butt."

Arthur nodded as he shuffled along the side of the road. He looked down the street and saw the ocean on the horizon, and toward the right, the lighthouse on the shore. Home. He thought for a moment about what was waiting for him there.

His dad. It was just him and his dad.

But he still felt like he was all alone.

"It's okay, you know," Claudia added. Arthur turned his head slightly to the right, cocking it, looking at Claudia as if to say, *What are you talking about?*

"Not having a mom. I don't have a mom."

"You don't?" Arthur asked.

Claudia shook her head, then shrugged. "It's okay."

Arthur kicked a rock down the middle of

the road. "I didn't know about your mom," Arthur said. "I'm sorry."

Claudia smiled. "I'm sorry about your mom, too."

Then Claudia stepped in front of Arthur and kicked the next rock before he had a chance.

"I was going to kick that," Arthur said.

"I know," Claudia replied.

CHAPTER
SIX

"THOSE STOMPING FEET CAN ONLY
mean one thing—someone must be here
to steal the beacon! The ships are doomed!
Doooooooooomed!"

Arthur sighed. That was one of his dad's
favorite jokes. Every time he trudged up the
stairs making heavy footsteps, and didn't
call out, *Hey, Dad, it's Arthur,* Tom would
make the joke. This had been going on for
years.

It wasn't very funny. At least, Arthur
didn't think so.

As he clomped up the spiraling steps toward the lighthouse beacon, Arthur looked down at his feet, and the well-worn boots, and shrugged his shoulders. "Hey, Dad, it's Arthur," he said, closing the loop on the father-son joke once again.

When he got to the top of the lighthouse, he saw Tom, wrench in hand, as he loosened a nut on the beacon assemblage. "Gotta make sure everything's working properly. Don't want any ships running into the dining room," Tom said, clearly in a good mood. "You done with your homework?" he asked.

Arthur nodded.

"Great. You ready to give your old man a hand?"

Arthur nodded again.

"Great. You gonna nod until your head falls off and rolls all the way down the stairs?"

Without thinking, Arthur nodded, then realized what his dad had just said. He managed a weak smile.

"You're here, but you aren't *here*, are you?"

Tom said. "Hand me that rag, will ya?"

Arthur reached inside his father's toolbox and grabbed an old rag spotted black with oil. He offered it to Tom.

"Anything in particular or everything in general?" Tom asked as he took the rag and wiped the oil off his hands.

"S'nothing," Arthur said, avoiding his father's eyes. "I don't want to talk about it."

Tom arched his back, then reached for the mug that was sitting on the floor near him and took a sip of coffee. "So, it's nothing, and you don't want to talk about it. Which means it's something," Tom said, looking at his son. "I have a crowbar somewhere around here. I suppose I could use that to pry it out of you. Might hurt a little."

Arthur managed a slight chuckle.

"What is it, kid?" Tom said, concern in his voice. "Something happen at school?"

Arthur shook his head. "Not at school."

"Field trip?"

Arthur nodded.

"Let me guess," Tom said, setting the cup of coffee down on the floor, and picking up a screwdriver. "Mike and Matt. Again."

"Sort of. A little. But not really, I guess," Arthur said.

Tom went to scratch the back of his head, stopping an instant before as he realized it was the hand that held the screwdriver. "I'm confused. So . . . what happened, exactly?"

"When we were at the aquarium, Mike and Matt were busting on me like usual," Arthur started. "And Matt pushed me up against a tank."

"Did he hurt you?" Tom asked, a note of anger creeping into his voice.

"No, he— It's hard to explain," Arthur said.

Tom took a breath. "Give me a shot."

For the first time since he'd entered the lighthouse, Arthur looked at his dad. "I was staring at the fish in the tank, and . . . I . . . I felt something."

"What do you mean?"

"I don't know. It was just a . . . feeling. I can't really explain it. And then all the fish were watching me."

Tom looked at his son sharply. "Watching you? What do you mean, watching you?"

Arthur nodded. "I mean they were watching me. They were all up against the glass just . . . looking at me. And . . . and when Matt shoved me against the tank, this shark . . . this shark sorta rammed into it."

"A shark rammed into the glass?" Tom asked. "That was just a coincidence, Arthur, you can't—"

"It hit the glass twice, Dad. In the same spot. It wasn't a coincidence, it . . . it was . . . weird. The shark actually cracked the glass," Arthur said. His voice was trembling.

"Are you okay?" Tom moved next to Arthur, holding his son by the shoulders, looking at him as if checking for wounds. "Are you hurt?"

"No, I'm not hurt, I'm just . . . ," Arthur replied, his voice trailing off. "It's like . . . I don't know, it's like, somehow, the fish, and me . . . like I could feel what they were feeling? And like they knew how I was feeling or something. Like they were . . . like they were trying to protect me. That's what it felt like, anyway."

For the next minute, neither father nor son said a word. Tom stood there, holding his son.

Then, at last, Arthur said, "I'm sorry."

"Why are you sorry? You have nothing to be sorry about," Tom said. "I'm the one who's sorry. Sorry that you have to go through this. Sorry that I can't do anything to make it easier for you."

"I just . . . They call me a freak, and I . . . I don't want to be a freak. I just want to be a kid."

"You *are* just a kid, Arthur," Tom said, trying to console his son. "But you're also something more. You're just . . . different, that's all."

"I don't want to be different," Arthur said.

"Different hurts."

"We are what we are," Tom said. "And part of you comes from me, and part of you comes from your mother. The things that made her different are what make you different, too."

"I don't want to be different!" Arthur yelled, the force of his voice surprising his father.

Tom looked at his son, eyes full of sympathy, struggling to find the right words. "Your mother loved you very much, Arthur. Seeing you, listening to you talk . . . it's like part of her is here with me, right now. I wish she could be here to help."

"If she loved me . . . if she loved you so much, why isn't she here now?" Arthur said bitterly.

Stunned silence followed as Arthur stormed out of the lighthouse.

CHAPTER
SEVEN

HE KICKED A ROCK, TAKING A CLUMP

of wet sand with it. The rock shot out toward the ocean, inches above the surface, before hitting the water and sinking with a tiny *plop.*

"Dang," Arthur said, realizing that he had gotten sand inside his boot in the process. "Now I'm a jerk *and* I have sand in my boot."

Why did I say that to Dad? Arthur wondered. *I shouldn't have. It's not his fault Mom left. It's not his fault, right?*

He stopped walking along the beach and

sat down in the sand. Untying his boots, he took them off and removed his socks. He stuffed them inside the boots, then tied the laces from one boot to another. Standing up, he slung the shoelace strap over his shoulder, and started to walk again, this time closer to the ocean. Close enough so the rolling tidewater would come in and cover his feet.

Gazing out into the distance, he saw the rocks that lined the shallows. When the tide-went out, you could walk to the rocks and sit on them. And when the water rolled back in, they would be covered again. Right now, they were partially visible.

He walked closer to the rocks, trying to clear his mind, which proved next to impossible. Arthur couldn't stop replaying the conversation with his father over in his head. And he couldn't stop thinking about what had happened at the aquarium. What was happening? What was going on? Why did everything have to be so, so . . . difficult?

Arthur heard the sound of splashing

water. It was almost like nature responding to his internal dialogue, the splash punctuating his unspoken sentence.

Then came another splash.

Then another.

"Hey, Topo," Arthur said, though there was no one else to be seen.

No one else, except a small octopus. The creature pulled itself out from the ocean, and onto one of the rocks in the shallows. Arthur now stood about ten feet away from the octopus, and he smiled at it. "Haven't seen you in a while," Arthur said out loud. "You been busy with octopus stuff?"

The octopus sat on the rock, minding its own business, splashing a tentacle in the water.

"All the time I talk, you just splash," Arthur said, starting to walk again. "It's like you're an octopus or something." The octopus slid off the rock, back into the water. Topo kept pace with Arthur, using its tentacles to scoot along in the shallow water, as Arthur walked.

"I don't know what's happening, Topo," Arthur said. "I mean, we've always been friends, since I can remember. But what happened today at the aquarium was . . . super creepy."

Looking over his shoulder, Arthur saw Topo splashing in the water. Maybe he saw something good to eat?

"I don't know, maybe I thought I was just some kind of . . . octopus whisperer or something. Seeing all those fish just floating there like that . . . and then the shark. I mean, the shark was seriously frightening."

Arthur jumped in the air and stamped down into the sand, squishing it between his toes. "But it wasn't frightening, y'know?"

Splash.

"The shark . . . the shark didn't look like it wanted to hurt me," Arthur said, thinking out loud now. "It looked like it wanted to hurt Matt. And Mike, I guess. It was like the shark was trying to protect me somehow."

Splash. Splash.

"I know, weird, right? And . . . I keep having these dreams. There are sharks in the
dream," Arthur said slowly.

Splash.

"The sharks, they don't hurt me or anything. They're just . . . there. I don't know
what's going on, Topo. I just . . . I just . . . ,"
Arthur said, grasping at the words.

He was quiet for a moment, then Arthur
turned to look at Topo. Arthur stopped walking, and Topo stopped scooting through the
water. The two remained there, in silence,
regarding one another, until Arthur said, "I
am telling my problems to an octopus."

CHAPTER
EIGHT

BY THE TIME ARTHUR ARRIVED AT the front door of his house, it was dark. He had been out on the beach for a few hours, long enough for him to lose track of time. He clasped the doorknob in his right hand, turning it slowly, trying not to make any noise. So far, so good. But when he pushed the door open, it creaked loudly.

Busted.

Not that he would have been able to sneak in anyway. His father was sitting there at the kitchen table, waiting for him, his omnipresent mug of coffee in front of him.

"Your dinner's in the oven," Tom said, not looking up from his coffee. "I kept it warm for you."

Arthur gave his head a little nod. "Thanks." He closed the door behind him, then walked over to the sink, washing his hands. Then he opened the oven door. Inside was a foil-wrapped plate. He removed the plate using a pot holder, then set it down on the table. Sitting down next to his dad, Arthur removed the foil. Meat loaf and mashed potatoes, with a side of green beans. There was a napkin on the table, along with a fork. He unfolded the paper napkin and put it on his lap, then took the fork in his right hand.

"Thanks, Dad," Arthur said softly.

"Sea fork," Tom replied, pointing at the utensil in Arthur's hand.

Arthur managed a smile.

He cut off a piece of meat loaf, then set his fork down. "I'm sorry. About before, I shouldn't . . . I was mean," Arthur said.

"It's okay," Tom said, his voice calm and low.

"No, I was mean, and I shouldn't have been. And then I came home late, and missed dinner, and—"

"It's okay, Arthur," Tom said, putting his hand on Arthur's. "I understand. I get it. If I were in your shoes, I'd probably have reacted the same way."

"My shoes are full of sand," Arthur said.

"Yeah, well, a hazard of living on the beach," Tom replied.

Arthur raised the fork to his mouth and took a bite of meat loaf. "S'good," he said, mouth full of food.

"Maybe it's time," Tom said.

"Time for what?" Arthur asked, taking a forkful of mashed potatoes.

"Time that you knew a little more about your mom," Tom said. "And why she really had to leave."

Arthur put the fork down and stared at his father. "Why did she leave?" he asked.

"I told myself that you had to be old enough; that's why I haven't shared everything. But if you're not old enough now, I don't know when you'll be old enough. Finish your dinner, and we'll talk."

They sat on the couch, the photo album spread out on the small coffee table in front of them. There was a baby picture of Arthur. A photo of his father. Then a picture of Tom with Arthur's mother, Atlanna. Then, finally, a photograph of Atlanna holding baby Arthur.

"I wish you could remember her," Tom said.

"I wish I could, too," Arthur echoed. "But I don't understand . . ."

"It was to protect you," Tom began. "To protect us. Your mother . . . your mother was . . . is . . . a queen."

"A queen?" Arthur asked, incredulous.

"A queen. Of Atlantis. But she found happiness here, with me. With you," Tom said, his voice growing smaller.

"Atlantis?" Arthur asked quietly. "Like . . . city-under-the-sea Atlantis?"

Tom nodded. "Continent, actually," he said softly. "That's where your mother is from. She wanted to stay here. With us. Forever. But she knew she couldn't."

"Why couldn't she?" His question sounded so innocent.

"Her people wouldn't let her," Tom said. "They would do anything to take her back. And if anyone got in their way? Well, they'd get rid of them."

"You mean you and me," Arthur said flatly.

"You and me," Tom answered. "They came for her once. Not many, just a few."

"Who were they?" Arthur asked.

"Her people," Tom said. "Atlanteans. They were soldiers. Trained to fight. But she was able to stop them, your mother was. She knew there would be more of them, though. Lots more. And if she didn't leave, they would take away everything she loved."

Arthur stared at the picture of his mom holding him. "But she had everything taken away from her anyway."

Tom rubbed his chin thoughtfully. "But at least we're alive, Arthur."

"At least," Arthur said.

CHAPTER NINE

HE COULDN'T BREATHE.

His lungs felt like they were going to explode from the inside. From the outside, he felt incredible pressure, like someone had placed a stack of bricks on his chest and decided to jump up and down on them.

Arthur felt a tugging sensation all around him, like he was being pulled in all directions at once. Was something there? And where was he? It was so dark, he couldn't see. Then he realized it was *water*. The water was yanking him this way and that, its strong current pulling Arthur along. And then Arthur knew where he was.

He was in the ocean again.

He tried to swim, to break free of the current, but it was no use. The current was too strong, and it yanked him along, deeper and deeper. Arthur tried to scream out, but there was no sound. He sucked water in and started to panic.

This isn't like before, Arthur thought. *The ocean's always been peaceful to me, but this . . . this . . . It's like I'm being attacked!*

Why was the ocean trying to take him? No matter what Arthur did, no matter how hard he struggled and kicked his legs, he couldn't seem to break free of the current. Deeper and deeper he went, eyes glancing upward at the tiny pinprick of light that he could see, and even that was now fading into distant memory.

This isn't like before . . .

His muscles ached like crazy, and he just wanted to close his eyes.

You can't! Don't stop!

Dragged along with the current, Arthur saw something in the murky depths moving up ahead.

Shark?

The shape seemed to be swimming, moving, back and forth, back and forth. What it was, Arthur couldn't tell. He strained his eyes, feeling like they might pop right out of his head. But he still couldn't see what it was.

His chest hurt. He desperately needed to breathe.

But he couldn't. And his body felt so heavy. So, so heavy . . .

The shape swam closer to Arthur, but it was still so hard to see. What was it? He reached out with his arms, trying to scoop the water, to pull himself toward the shape. It looked vaguely human. There was something about it . . . something that seemed safe? Arthur couldn't understand why he felt that way.

The shape was coming closer, closer than it had before, and Arthur swore he could see that the shape had . . . a face? Long hair swirled around the shape's face, and as Arthur looked, he saw beautiful, strong features. The shape seemed to smile at Arthur.

I know that face . . . I've seen it before . . .

Then Arthur screamed, "Mother!"

The sound didn't travel, and the shape didn't respond. As he screamed, Arthur gulped in a lungful of water; he felt light-headed, his chest burned, and his whole body felt heavy. So, so heavy. He screamed again, but this time, he began to gag.

And as everything turned black, he swore he heard a soft voice . . . "Arthur."

Arthur's scream had woken Tom out of a dead sleep, and he had come running to his son's room. He found Arthur sitting bolt upright, his pajama shirt soaking wet, sticking to his back. Sweat poured down his forehead.

And yet, Arthur felt decidedly cold to the touch.

"Same dream?" Tom asked, sitting on the side of his son's bed.

Arthur shook his head. "Sort of. But it was different. I think I saw Mom," Arthur said, panting.

"You saw her?" Tom asked.

Arthur nodded. "I think it was her. I tried . . . I tried to call out to her, but I was drowning, I couldn't breathe, and I just wanted . . . I just wanted to talk to her."

Tom looked at his son and started to say something. *It's like he's trying to find the words*, Arthur thought, *but can't*. Then Tom pulled Arthur close to him and wrapped the boy in an embrace.

Then, a few seconds later, "I just want you to know that you're really sweaty and gross right now."

Arthur managed to laugh.

Tom rose from the bed and walked over to Arthur's closet, and the two piles of clothes that sat on the floor in front of it. He looked at the pile on the left, then bent down and grabbed a blue "Amnesty Bay" T-shirt. "Pile on the left is the clean pile, right?" Tom said.

Arthur nodded, and Tom threw the shirt to his son. "Put that on; you're cold. And don't th—"

Arthur took off the sweaty shirt, then threw it on the floor.

"—row it on the floor," Tom said, completing his thought, laughing. "One day, you'll learn."

Tom walked back to the bed. "You gonna be okay?"

"I think so." Arthur yawned. "What time is it?"

"Three thirty in the morning, give or take," Tom replied. "Get some sleep. You got school tomorrow."

Tom messed up the hair on his son's head, then left the room. Then there was quiet, then Arthur was alone once more.

He turned in bed and closed his eyes, hoping he would see her face again.

CHAPTER
TEN

"ARE WE BORING YOU, ARTHUR?"

Arthur suddenly snapped to, jerking his head off his desk. He wiped a thin stream of drool from the right corner of his mouth.

Man, I hope no one saw that, he thought. Then he looked around at his classmates and realized that everyone probably had seen it.

"I'm sorry, Mrs. Lewis," Arthur said apologetically. "I didn't get a lot of sleep last night."

Mrs. Lewis stood at the board in front of

the classroom and gave Arthur a sympathetic smile. "Just try not to snore next time," she said, and the class laughed.

Laughing at me, not with me, Arthur thought.

"Now, where were we?" Mrs. Lewis continued. "We were talking about the difference between mass and weight . . ." Then she began to draw a diagram on the SMART Board.

Arthur felt a finger poke him in his right shoulder. He turned his head slightly, and saw Claudia leaning over from her desk.

"What's up with you?" Claudia whispered. "You look terrible."

Arthur shrugged. "I just didn't get much sleep," he replied in a hushed voice. Arthur shifted his body, and lifted his head, looking up at the white board, full of words and diagrams that made his head hurt. He tried to focus, but he had that eerie feeling of being stared at. He slowly swiveled his head to the right, and sure enough, he saw Claudia, still

looking right at him.

"I don't believe you," Claudia whispered. "C'mon, what is it?"

"I don't want to talk about it right now!" Arthur whispered back.

"Try to keep the noise to a dull roar," Mrs. Lewis said, her back to the class as she wrote on the board.

"C'mon, I don't want to get in trouble," Arthur said softly.

Then he felt something wet and slimy strike his neck from behind, and he gasped. Arthur reached around with his right hand and pulled out a small, curled-up piece of paper, soaking wet.

Classic spit wad, he thought.

He turned around in his seat and saw Matt and Mike waving at him. Matt held a straw in one hand, wiggling it. Mike was busy rolling up bits of paper into tiny balls. Matt took one of the balls, popped it in his mouth. Then he took it out, put it in the front of the straw, and fired again.

Arthur tried to duck, but the spit wad caught him right in the cheek.

Yecccch.

Arthur couldn't believe how the day was turning out so far. He wanted to get up out of his seat and go after Matt. Inside, he felt his stomach churning, and he clenched his fists beneath his desk. But he knew if he did anything, he'd get in trouble. He knew his father would be disappointed in him for picking a fight. And if he told Mrs. Lewis, he'd be the class snitch and then everyone would dislike him more than they already did.

"That's great," Arthur said. "Now Matt and Mike have another reason to hate my guts."

It was lose-lose all the way around.

"Hey!"

Arthur whirled around to see Matt covering his right eye with his hands. Then he pulled them away, revealing a little wad of wet paper stuck above his right eyebrow.

"What is going on here?" Mrs. Lewis

thundered. "Claudia, what on earth are you doing?"

Arthur looked at Claudia and couldn't believe what he saw. There she was, half sitting in her seat, turned backward, a straw in hand.

"Spit-wad fight? Really?" Mrs. Lewis asked the class, incredulous.

"They started it!" Claudia said, pointing at Matt and Mike.

"I did not!" Matt said, wiping the spit wad off his face.

"Me neither!" Mike added. "We're totally innocent! This is a witch hunt!"

Mrs. Lewis rolled her eyes. "Uh-huh, I bet. Straws on the floor, now. Both of you," she said, and both Matt and Claudia complied. "I'll be seeing the three of you after class."

"But Mrs. Lewis—" Arthur started to say, surprising himself.

"What, Arthur?" Mrs. Lewis replied. "Would you like to stay after class, too?"

Claudia put a hand on Arthur's shoulder. "No, Arthur, it's fine, don't worry about it. What are friends for?"

Arthur looked at his friend and smiled.

CHAPTER
ELEVEN

ARTHUR LOOKED UP AT THE SKY and felt the warmth of the sun on his face. He felt dazed, like he was floating an inch or so off the ground, and everything looked and felt fuzzy to him.

I gotta get some sleep, he thought.

He heard the sound of the school doors opening behind him, and Arthur stood up from his seat on the concrete steps. Claudia came walking out of the school, backpack slung over her left shoulder.

"Hey, stranger," she said, waving to Arthur.

Arthur waved back. "Hey," he replied. "I'm really sorry about before. I didn't want you to get in tr—"

"Pffffft," Claudia said. "Don't worry about it. Those jerks had it coming. Besides, Mrs. Lewis knows what's going on. Believe me, I got a slap on the wrist compared to the punishment those two geniuses got."

Arthur raised an eyebrow as if to say, *Do tell*.

"They'll be staying after school for the next month or so," Claudia said, relishing every word that came out of her mouth.

"Doing what?" Arthur asked.

"I believe Mrs. Lewis's exact words were 'assisting the custodian in the fulfillment of his daily duties,'" Claudia said, giggling.

"That's great," Arthur said, hanging his head. "Now Matt and Mike have another reason to hate my guts. Not like they needed it."

"You worry too much," Claudia said. "I got your back."

Arthur thought for a second, then smiled. "What about you?"

"I have to help Mrs. Lewis plan a lesson next week," Claudia said, a big grin on her face.

"So basically, something you would have volunteered to do," Arthur said, shaking his head.

Claudia laughed. "Basically. What can I say, things always seem to work out."

They walked down the steps together and headed out into the parking lot.

"Our dads are probably worried about us," Claudia said. "Y'know, 'cause it's so late."

Arthur thought about that for a second and shrugged. "My dad won't mind. He's cool about stuff like that. And it's not like I have any chores today or anything."

"'Chores'?" Claudia asked, her tone slightly mocking. "What is this, *Little House on the Prairie*?"

Arthur laughed. "Okay, then what should I call them? It's just fixing stuff around the lighthouse, maintaining the beacon, stuff like that."

Claudia nodded. "Sounds cool. All I ever get to do is take out garbage and dust. You wouldn't believe how dusty our house is. It's, like, *made* of dust or something."

They walked through the parking lot and onto the grass, to the road beyond.

"Well, thanks for waiting for me and stuff," Claudia said.

"Sure. What are friends for?" Arthur replied, and Claudia smiled.

"It was pretty cool what you did," Arthur said. "With the straw. The spit-wad thing."

Claudia laughed. "Thanks. A necessary skill."

"You'll have to teach me," Arthur said. "I have to be able to defend myself."

Claudia looked at Arthur. "Are you telling me that you and your dad have never had a spit-wad fight?"

Arthur shook his head. "No way! Are you kidding? I mean, he's fun and all, but I just don't think Tom Curry is the spitwad-fight type."

"Too bad," Claudia replied. "You guys are missing out."

Hefting his backpack onto his right shoulder, Arthur shifted its weight. He and Claudia were walking through downtown Amnesty Bay, passing the numerous small businesses that dotted the well-worn, pothole-filled street.

"Do you ever think about your mom?" Arthur asked slowly.

Claudia didn't say anything, and she didn't look up. They just kept on walking. Then, after a while, she said, "Sometimes. A lot of times. I mean, I can't help it. It's hard not to miss her."

Arthur nodded. "I know," he said quietly.

"I know you know," Claudia responded. "Why do you ask?"

"I had a dream about my mom last night,"

Arthur said. "At least, I think it was my mom. I couldn't really tell."

"I bet it was your mom," Claudia said.

"How do you know?" Arthur inquired. "I mean, I don't know, and I'm the one who had the dream."

"It wouldn't be bothering you so much if it were someone else," Claudia said.

She's probably right, Arthur thought.

"I don't really remember her," he said, kicking a rock with his sneaker. "I was too young. Do you remember yours?"

Claudia stopped, then lined up a rock in front of her right foot. Then she gave it a kick with her hiking boot, sending the rock at least twice as far as Arthur's rock. "You gotta get behind it," she said. Then, "A little. I was really young when my mom died. Like, four."

"I was three when my mom left," Arthur said.

"That sucks," Claudia said.

"Yeah."

"Race you to the beach?" Claudia asked, and before Arthur could answer, she was already off and running.

Maybe it doesn't suck so bad, Arthur thought.

CHAPTER
TWELVE

HE STILL COULDN'T BREATHE.

But now, *now* he could see the shape's face, more clearly than ever before.

It *was* his mother.

Only this time, Arthur didn't try to call out to her. He didn't want his lungs to fill with water. The current was there, and just like last time, it was pulling at him from all sides, but this time, he resisted. This time, he swam, harder than he had before, and at last he moved forward, if just a little. Then a little more. He was making progress. Arthur was coming closer to the shape, closer and closer.

I know it's her, I just know it. I can feel it.

The shape reached out its arms, beckoning toward Arthur. He was only inches from her embrace. When he saw her, Arthur suddenly jerked backward, as if yanked by an unseen force. The shape appeared just as surprised as Arthur.

No, they can't take her away. Not again. I won't let them!

Arthur swam after his mother, keeping pace with her, yet she always remained just out of reach. His muscles ached, and he thought his chest would burst, but Arthur refused to relent. Stroke after stroke, he soldiered on, striving with all his might to keep close to his mother.

Arthur was so preoccupied that he only then noticed that he was just a few feet above the ocean floor. Up ahead he saw a ridge. A second later, his mother disappeared over the ridge, heading down.

That's where I'm going, too.

Arthur surprised himself with how easy it was to swim now, as if the current wasn't fighting his every move or latching and grabbing at him. He made it to the ridge and saw nothing beyond except darkness. Then he hurled himself downward, and he found himself sinking like a rock. His mother was still, agonizingly, just out of reach.

All around him, Arthur noticed it growing darker and darker. And yet, up ahead, there was a strange, almost unearthly glow. It was small but appeared to grow larger as he swam on.

What is it? Where are they taking her?

His mother turned slowly, her hair finally revealing her face. She looked at Arthur and mouthed a word.

Home? Did she say "home"?

And then he saw what was making the unearthly glow. Behind the shape, Arthur saw what looked like a city. If that's in fact what it was, for it resembled no city that

Arthur had ever seen or heard of before. The architecture was different from anything he had experienced in Amnesty Bay, or anywhere else, for that matter. Great stone-like columns rose from the ocean floor, spanning upward. It was a city that couldn't have existed above the waves. It was hard to believe he was still on Earth.

What is this place?

As Arthur treaded water, he became aware of a peculiar sensation. The ocean current seemed to stop, and the water around him became still.

Then there came a low rumbling sound. Small at first, and Arthur looked around, trying to place it. He looked at his mother swimming closer. She smiled at Arthur, but there was something sad in her eyes.

The moment between them passed. The mild rumble grew louder and louder, and closer, until Arthur finally saw just what the rumbling was: a wave, moving through the water itself, heading directly for Arthur. It was impossible, Arthur knew, and yet it was happening right before his eyes.

The wave crashed toward Arthur, and at last the boy screamed as it overcame him, pummeling his body.

As his lungs filled with water, Arthur was carried away by the force of the wave. He kept on screaming, as futile a gesture as it was, reaching out for his mother.

His mother looked at Arthur mournfully, and as the wave dragged him away, she became smaller and smaller.

"For the record, it's three thirty a.m. Again," Tom said.

"Give or take," Arthur replied, panting.

"Are you okay?" Tom asked, concern in his voice. "I . . . What can I do?"

"I'm fine, Dad," Arthur said, putting his head back down on his pillow. "It's not . . . It's just a dream, that's all."

"Arthur," Tom said softly. "Your mom . . .

your mom had dreams, too. Some of them very real. She thought . . . maybe they were omens of the future. Or echoes of the past."

"Dreams about what?" Arthur asked.

Tom was silent for a moment. "She didn't want to talk much about them," he said. "But I think they were of her family. Her father."

"Do *you* think they were omens?"

Tom scratched his head. "I'm not sure, kid," he said. "It's all a little beyond me. But I loved your mom. And if she believed it, well, then I bet there might be something to it."

Arthur nodded and sat there in bed, staring upward.

"You sure you don't wanna talk?"

"I'm sure," Arthur said.

"I know it's hard to believe right now," Tom said, "but everything's gonna be all right. We're gonna make it all right."

Arthur didn't say anything.

CHAPTER
THIRTEEN

"YOU CALL *THAT* A BICYCLE?"

Arthur stared down at the bike beneath his legs, pumping furiously to keep up. He'd spent the better part of yesterday afternoon working on the gears, oiling the chain, but there was no way around it. The bike was old, a little beat-up, and not in the best of shape.

Not like Claudia's bike. She worked like crazy to keep it in good working condition. After all, it was absolutely necessary for a thirteen-year-old with a paper route to have the best bike possible.

They had spent the mornings of the last few weeks the same way, ever since school let out for the summer. Arthur had mentioned that he was going to get a paper route to earn some extra money, apart from all the chores he did around the lighthouse. Claudia said (impossibly, it seemed to Arthur) that it sounded like fun, and that she would get one, too.

So they did.

And now Claudia was outpedaling Arthur as they rode down the main street of Amnesty Bay, each with a sack of newspapers slung low over the handlebars of their bikes.

"I do call this a bicycle," Arthur said, riding just behind Claudia. "It's my bicycle."

Claudia laughed. "I'm just teasing," she said. "Your bike is pretty cool. It's been through a lot. Like it has a story to tell."

"Yeah, if it could talk, it would say, 'Arthur crashed me into lots of stuff before falling off of me.'"

They both laughed at that one.

"How many papers you got left?" Arthur asked.

"Five," Claudia said. "Just the ones on Fradon Street. How about you?"

"Nine," Arthur replied. "What do you wanna do when we're done?"

"Did you hear about the octopus?" Claudia asked, an air of mystery in her voice.

Arthur cocked his head. "What octopus?"

"One of the local fishermen caught an octopus this morning. Big thing! Guess it had been raiding the lobster traps for food," Claudia said. She glanced over at Arthur, who had a strange look on his face. "Uh, you okay?"

"What? Yeah," Arthur said, feeling anything but okay. "I'm . . . I just forgot I have something I gotta do. I'll catch ya later, Claudia."

"Arthur, wait—"

But before she could say another word, Arthur had already turned his bicycle around, racing down to the docks.

"Get a load o' this guy!"

Arthur's bike skidded to a stop on the dock, and he couldn't believe the sight that awaited him. There was the local fisherman that Claudia had been talking about, Gilly. He was standing in front of a large, water-filled tank. It was easily eight feet long, like the kind of tanks that restaurants would use to display all kinds of colorful saltwater fish. Several people from town were crowding around it, and Arthur's stomach sank when he saw that both Matt and Mike were among them.

He hit the kickstand with his left foot and parked the bike just beyond the crowd. Then he ran over to the tank, pushing his way through the crowd.

"Hey!"

"Watch it!"

"You'll get your turn!"

But Arthur didn't hear the voices. He was

too intent on seeing exactly what was inside the tank.

Or rather, who.

Topo . . .

The octopus was bigger than some of the largest fishermen in Amnesty Bay. It had the same markings as the one that Arthur had first seen when he was just a little kid. The one that always seemed to walk along the shore with him. The one that Arthur would talk to, the one that always listened to whatever Arthur had to say.

Arthur shoved his way to the front of the crowd, until he was right next to the tank. The people looked at him as if to say, *Who does he think he is?* but said nothing. Arthur placed a hand on the glass, and the octopus responded instantly, placing one of its tentacles against Arthur's hand from the other side.

"I guess you guys are family," Matt said, chuckling in his own inimitable, not-too-smart way.

Mike followed suit, laughing.

Arthur gave a steadfast look to Gilly. "You have to let it go."

Gilly was a great big man, over six feet tall, with curly red hair, and he was missing his two front teeth. He smiled at Arthur and said, "Now, why would I do that, kid? I caught a perfectly good octopus! Look at it! What a prize!"

"It's not a prize," Arthur said. "Let it go!"

"Look, kid," Gilly said, trying to sound sympathetic. He leaned down to face Arthur eye to eye, resting his hands on his knees. "I know, it's about conservation or preservation or whatever, right? I'm gonna sell the octopus to the aquarium, make a little extra money, and this octopus will live in the lap of luxury. It'll get all the food it wants, and you can visit it on weekends, okay?"

"Awwww, you gonna miss da widdle octopus?" Mike said, giving Arthur a little shove.

But by then, Arthur had stopped paying attention. He had a weird feeling again.

Just like at the aquarium, he thought.

"Are you all right?"

Arthur snapped out of it, turned, and saw Claudia.

She must have followed me.

"I . . . don't know," he said, and Claudia shook her head.

"What's going on, Arthur?"

Arthur didn't answer. He felt the strange feeling inside his head again, as he cast his eyes upward, and looked at Topo.

Topo hates it. I know Topo hates it.

The feeling seemed to hit Arthur from all sides, and he held his temples with his hands. He felt Claudia put an arm around him, pulling him away from the tank. But Arthur yanked back, refusing to leave Topo's side. Through the tank, in the ocean, Arthur could see a fishing boat coming into port, carrying its fresh catch.

Turning to the left, Arthur saw two other fishing boats returning on the opposite side of the dock. Their nets were full of fish.

The feeling inside his head grew until Arthur could barely stand it.

Arthur held his head and gritted his teeth.

What is this pain? I've never felt anything like this before—

"Arthur?" Claudia said, looking into Arthur's eyes. "You don't look so good."

Claudia grabbed his arm, and suddenly, Arthur got an idea. He grabbed Claudia's arm back and pulled in close to her ear. "I'm gonna do something, and I want you to just go with it," he said.

Claudia shot him a look that said, "Uh, say WHAT?!"

"Oooooohhhhhhh!" Arthur moaned. He grabbed his stomach, and then promptly hurled himself to the dock in front of the tank and started to moan even louder. "OOHHH-HHHHHH! I think I'm gonna be sick!"

He might as well have been inside a crowded movie theater and yelled, *Fire*. The crowd suddenly parted around him, horri-fied at the thought that this kid might boot all over the dock.

Arthur rolled over on his side and looked up, seeing the crowd that was now pushing to get away from him. Arthur continued to moan, holding his belly, making burbling sounds from his mouth that made everyone try to run even faster.

Gilly looked at Arthur, then at Claudia, concerned. "Is this kid all right?" Gilly asked Claudia, who shrugged. "He doesn't sound all right. I had a dog that made sounds like that whenever he got sick. It was the worst!"

Rolling over a little more, he saw Topo in the tank, arms thrashing wildly.

What is Topo waiting for? Arthur thought. *Get outta here!*

And as everyone focused on Arthur, the tank behind them started to rock, back and forth. Back and forth, as the octopus within threw its tentacles and its mass against one side of the tank, and then the other, back and forth.

"What the hell?!" Gilly shouted.

Back and forth, the tank rocked, until it flipped over into the ocean.

Arthur could hear Gilly cursing as he saw Topo flee from the tank and make its way out to sea.

Good job, Topo.

"Are you okay, Arthur?" Claudia said, cradling Arthur's head, barely suppressing a smile.

"I . . . I think I'll live," Arthur said, pretending to pass out.

Claudia leaned over him and whispered in his ear, "Worst. Performance. Ever."

CHAPTER
FOURTEEN

"YOU'RE NOT GONNA WIN AN
Oscar any time soon."

Arthur sat on the beach, looking straight up at the overcast sky. His eyes focused in on two seagulls flying up above, circling. And he saw Claudia, sitting on the sand right next to him, shaking her head.

"Are. You. Okay?" she asked, each word a sentence unto itself.

"Yeah," Arthur said, squishing the sand between his toes. "I mean, I'm not gonna really vomit, if that's what you mean."

"Yeah, I kinda figured that out from your amazing performance," Claudia joked. "It was terrible, but I think everyone else bought it hook, line, and sinker. Which is unbelievable."

"I'm surprised they all believed it," Arthur said, standing up slowly. "But who's gonna take a chance and get ralphed on?"

He looked past Claudia and saw their bikes ditched in the sand. He saw a set of footprints leading over to the spot upon which they sat, and another set of marks that looked like someone dragging someone else.

"I can't believe I literally dragged you away from the dock," Claudia said. "Literally."

"I literally believe it," Arthur replied, managing a weak smile.

"When you pretended to pass out, couldn't you have 'woken up' sooner?"

"Sorry," Arthur said, grinning. "I had to sell it. I couldn't just walk away, not after that."

"You're some kinda weird," Claudia said.

"But I like that." She looked away from Arthur, and at the ocean.

Then Arthur did the same.

"So, what *really* happened?" Claudia said. "One minute, you're arguing with Gilly about the octopus, and the next, you're acting all weird, and then you're pretending like you're gonna hurl all over the crowd."

Arthur shrugged his shoulders. He started to speak, and then he stopped.

"What?" Claudia asked, her eyes staring into his. "You can tell me. Remember: spit-wad affair? You owe me."

Arthur tried to chuckle, but only a tiny sound came out. "I'm . . . I'm gonna tell you something," Arthur said deliberately, "and it's kinda weird. Like, really weird. So you have to promise that you won't, like, run away or anything."

"You're not like a serial killer, are you?" Claudia joked, scooting backward in the sand.

"What?" Arthur replied, taking it seriously

for about a half second. "No! No, just . . . no! Nothing like that. But it's . . . it's hard to put into words and probably harder to believe it."

Claudia felt the tiny grains of sand beneath her hands and started to draw circles. "You can say whatever you want; I'm not going anywhere."

Taking a deep breath, Arthur nodded. "Okay. Well, back there at the dock? That octopus? I . . . *know* that octopus," he began.

"You *know* that octopus," Claudia repeated, her face and voice both monotone. "Like *know* know him? Like a friend? What is he, like, your pet or something?"

"No, not my pet octopus. Topo doesn't belong to me. It doesn't belong to anyone," Arthur said.

"Topo?" Claudia asked.

"Yeah, I call it Topo."

"Right . . . *Topo*," Claudia said, as she continued to draw in the sand. "Because that's like a traditional octopus name or something."

"Anyway. There's, like, this . . . connection between me and Topo. It's like I can feel whatever it is that it is feeling. And I think . . . ," Arthur said, his voice trailing off.

"You think what?" Claudia said, looking at his eyes.

"I think . . . it can understand me."

Claudia stared at Arthur.

"You're gonna run away now, aren't you?" Arthur said.

"No, I'm not. So Topo . . . understands you?"

"Yeah. Like, back there at the dock . . . I told it to get outta there. I mean, I didn't say it out loud, but I thought it."

Claudia kept drawing circles in the sand. She said nothing, and the sound of the incoming waves filled the air. Slowly, she began to speak. "The tank," she said.

"The tank," echoed Arthur.

"So you created a distraction, so Topo could escape?"

"Yep."

Arthur watched as Claudia continued to sketch in the sand.

"So?"

"So?" Claudia answered.

"So, aren't you gonna say something? Like, tell me I'm out of my mind?" Arthur ranted.

"I don't think you're out of your mind," Claudia said. "I believe you."

Arthur looked at Claudia.

Maybe Dad was right. Maybe everything will *be okay.*

CHAPTER
FIFTEEN

ARTHUR WAS SURPRISED BY THE gust of wind as he pedaled his bike home. It hit him from behind, pushing him forward down the worn street. Looking out over the ocean, he watched as the waves rolled in, cresting white, crashing into the rocky shore.

A minute or so later, and Arthur was home. The sun was setting, and he saw the lights on. He parked his bike, then opened the front door. Inside, he could hear people talking.

Company? Arthur thought, though that

seemed doubtful. He listened closely, leaning in.

"—likely to need more than a raincoat in the next few days."

Nope, it's just the TV.

Arthur walked into the living room, where his father was sitting on the edge of the couch, fixated on the TV. The local news station was turned on, and he was watching the weather. Arthur saw a big "Storm of the Century?" graphic imposed on the screen.

"Hey, Dad," Arthur said.

Tom didn't say anything, but quickly raised his left hand, palm out, in a gesture that Arthur knew meant, "Quiet! I'm watching this!"

He plopped down next to his father and watched along with him. The weatherman was a curious-looking guy with slick black hair matted to his head, wearing an ill-fitting suit that looked like it had been the height of fashion in 1970. He spoke in a high-pitched voice, and Arthur wondered how a guy like this got on TV in the first place.

"The coastal storm is already developing, and if you've been outside at all in the last hour, you'll notice the high winds are already starting," the weatherman said, his voice squeaking. "The storm is expected to make landfall in the next twenty-four hours. Depending upon the route, the storm might slam right into Amnesty Bay. So now's the time to batten those hatches and tape those windows!"

Tom got up from the couch, walked over to the TV, and turned it off. "Big storm rolling in," he said gravely, looking at Arthur. "I've spent a good chunk of the day getting the lighthouse ready. If any fishing boats get caught out there tomorrow, we'll be ready. How are y— Arthur, what's wrong?"

I don't wanna tell him. I don't wanna tell him, Arthur thought.

"Nothing's wrong," Arthur lied.

Tom pointed a finger in Arthur's direction, shaking it. "I'm your father, and I can tell when something's wrong. The look on your face says it all," Tom said. "You're practically screaming, *Ask me what's going on, Dad.* Something happened today. What?"

"Dad, c'mon . . . I just got through telling all this to Claudia." Arthur hemmed and hawed.

"Claudia? The girl who has the paper route? The spit-wad champion of Amnesty Bay?"

Arthur rolled his eyes. "Yeah, Dad, that Claudia. Anyway, it's no big deal."

"I'll be the judge of that. You told Claudia; you can tell me. Out with it."

Sighing, Arthur leaned his head so it was draped over the back of the couch. "Fine," he said with a huff. "I was down at the dock today, and Gilly was showing off this octopus he caught."

Tom had a stupefied look on his face. "Gilly actually caught something?" he said, his voice tinged with disbelief.

Ignoring his father, Arthur continued, "It

was Topo, Dad. Gilly caught Topo. And I was so angry . . ."

"You mean the octopus? The one you talk to? What did you do, Arthur?" Tom asked, suddenly concerned. "Are you okay? Are you hurt?"

"No, it's nothing like that. I just . . . It's like I could hear it, Dad. I mean, it wasn't talking or anything, but it's like I could feel Topo in my head. I got mad. I mighta kinda sorta pretended to be sick so everyone would pay attention to me, and Topo ran."

"Octopi don't run," Tom prodded. "What happened?"

"Topo knocked over the tank and escaped into the ocean. It's like it understood me, Dad." For the first time since he got home, Arthur smiled.

Tom walked over to the couch and made a motion for Arthur to move over. He sat down next to his son and patted him on the knee.

"And it wasn't just with Topo," Arthur continued. "It was the fish. The fishermen? They came in with their catch. And it's like . . . I could feel them, too. They didn't want to be caught . . . They were in pain. And I could feel it. I wish I could have done something for them, too."

"I'm not surprised," Tom said softly. "I probably should be, but I'm not."

Arthur stared at his dad, wide-eyed. "How is that even possible?"

"We used to talk about this, your mother and I. You're unique, Arthur, you know this. You're half human and half Atlantean. She—your mother—thought that you might have . . . I guess you'd call them skills? Abilities? She said that as you got older, these . . . powers would show up, develop," Tom said, looking at Arthur.

The boy cast his eyes downward and didn't say anything. Tom kept going. "I don't know, Arthur, I'm just a lighthouse keeper. But your mother, she was amazing. And she knew with all her heart that one day you'd be able to do some pretty amazing things."

"Like what kind of amazing things?" Arthur said quietly.

"Hold that thought," Tom said. "I've got something to show you. Be right back."

With that, Tom pushed himself off the couch and walked briskly from the living room. Arthur looked up, not sure exactly what his father was doing. His eyes drifted over to the black screen of the TV. He wanted to turn it back on so he wouldn't have to talk about anything.

A minute later Tom returned with an old, well-worn, leather-covered book clasped in his hands. He offered it to Arthur. "Here, take this," Tom said, and Arthur did.

"What book is this?" Arthur asked, feeling the cover with his fingers. "It looks old." He ran his hand along the front cover and felt the wrinkled leather binding. The title of the book was stamped in gold foil—*The Mystery of Atlantis*, by Bernard Collins.

"It is old. I bought it a long time ago," Tom said. "Your mom and I would read it together. It's a guide to the myths and legends of Atlantis, its history. Your mom would tell me what was real and what was baloney. I think it's time that you read it and learn a little more about your mom. Who she was. Who you are."

Tom stopped talking abruptly, then wrung his hands together. "I'm sorry, Arthur, I'm not good at this kinda thing."

Arthur stared at his dad. "You're doing fine. We're both in 'uncharted water' here."

Tom sighed and smirked. "Arthur, remember what I told you about puns."

For the first time since he entered the house, Arthur smiled a little. "They're jokes for people who think they're funny. You know that's just not true, right?"

Tom shrugged. "Agree to disagree. Anyway. Your mother would have wanted you to have this, Arthur. Keep it safe. It's a piece of her that you can take with you wherever you go."

"She . . . ," Arthur said, struggling to find the words.

"She what?" Tom replied.

"Mom . . . She's never coming back, is she?"

Tom grew quiet, then took a deep breath and forced a smile. "It's getting late. Get some sleep," he said, then he left the room, leaving Arthur alone with his mother's book.

CHAPTER
SIXTEEN

"HOW MANY YOU GOT LEFT?"

With a broad smile, Arthur tugged the sides of the canvas bag apart, turned it upside down, and shook it. "None," he bragged. "I have NONE left. How about you?"

Claudia circled back on her bike, stopped pedaling, coasted, then hit the brakes. She came to a stop right in front of Arthur's bike. "Let me see that," she said, grabbing hold of the bag and peering inside. Claudia shoved her right hand into the bag, running it all around, touching all sides. "That's not possible. Does this thing have a trapdoor or something?"

"No, I finished! I swear!" Arthur said.

It was the first time all summer that Arthur had beaten Claudia on the paper route, and Claudia couldn't believe it. She stood astride her bike, feet planted on the ground, staring at Arthur's empty bag, dumbfounded. "I still have five papers left," she said, talking more to herself than to Arthur. "How. Is. This. Possible?"

"The universe works in mysterious ways," Arthur jabbed. "You wanna do something after you're done? Head over to May's, check out the comics?"

Claudia looked up at the gray sky. The storm clouds had been building all morning, and the winds had continued to strengthen overnight. An old tree next to the Amnesty Bay pharmacy had already lost a branch thanks to the wind, downing some power lines. But the rain and flooding were still to come.

"I dunno. The storm's supposed to be pretty bad," Claudia said. "You wanna watch movies or something?"

"Yeah, that'd be cool. You wanna come over?" Arthur said.

"Sure!" Claudia answered. "Just need to use the pay phone to call my dad and let him know."

Fifteen minutes later, Claudia had finished up her paper route. She and Arthur rode through downtown, where she stopped to use the pay phone at May's Pharmacy while Arthur browsed the comics.

When they had finished up, they hopped back on their bikes and rode toward the shore, on their way to the Curry house. A light rain started to fall, but Arthur didn't mind it. There was something about the droplets hitting his face that he liked.

Arthur looked down at the beach, watching the waves crash into the shore. The surf looked rough, and it was—the approaching storm saw to that. The water churned, foaming white at the top. He thought about Topo for a second. He hadn't seen Topo since the incident at the dock, and he hoped that the octopus would be okay with the storm and all.

It's an octopus, Arthur, he thought. *It lives in the water; it'll be fine. Knucklehead.*

"What are those idiots doing?"

Arthur whipped his head around to see Claudia riding next to him, staring out toward the ocean.

"What idiots?" Arthur asked.

Claudia pointed a finger toward the shoreline. "*Those* idiots!"

Arthur notice a group of kids on the beach, surrounding a catamaran. The boat sat on the wet sand, its twin hulls half in the water, half out.

"What kind of *brainiacs* take a boat out with the storm of the century coming our way?" Claudia asked. She squinted, then smacked her forehead with an open hand. "Of course it would be them."

Arthur squinted, too, and saw Matt and Mike.

Figures, he thought.

Matt and Mike were trying to push the catamaran into the oncoming waves, along with two other students that Arthur recognized from class—Nikki and a kid that everyone just knew as Peanut.

"I get that Matt and Mike would want to do something this dumb, and everyone knows that Peanut is a lost cause," Claudia ranted. "But Nikki? Shouldn't she know better?"

As if on cue, Nikki started to wave wildly. "Hey, guys! Give us a hand?" Nikki said, shouting over the wind.

"Rats," Claudia said. "Spotted." She stopped pedaling and let her bike come to a slow stop.

"We could just ignore 'em?" Arthur said, hitting the brakes. "Pretend we couldn't hear her? Or see her?"

"Yeah, give us some help getting this thing

in the water!" Matt bellowed. "Unless fish boy's afraid of getting wet!"

Arthur bit his lip, feeling anger welling up within him. Claudia noticed it, too. She put a hand on his shoulder.

"Ignore the jerk," Claudia said. "Let's just get to your place, and we can hang out and watch movies the rest of the day. I know you're dying to watch *The Blob* for the thirtieth time."

Arthur felt his anger subside a little. He knew Claudia was right.

"I don't know if you guys noticed or not, but there's kind of like a storm rolling in?" Arthur yelled over the sound of the wind. "Don't you think it's a little . . . not smart to be taking the boat out in weather like this?"

"Hey, it's Curry. Cool," said Peanut, nodding slowly, as if he were the only one who'd noticed that Arthur had arrived.

"Peanut," Arthur said. "Can't you guys wait until the storm is over to go out?"

Matt looked at Arthur, smiling. Then he

turned to Claudia. "Yeah, I'm not waiting for anything, especially not some dumb storm," he said, a snide tone in his voice. "Everyone get on the side of that hull and push."

"Yeah, I'm not pushing anything," Claudia said. "For the record, I think you're all a bunch of dopes. Why are you going out now? The storm's gonna hit soon. You wanna be lost at sea?"

Mike laughed. "Oh, come on. That guy on the TV doesn't know anything. He just sits there squawkin' in a weird voice, thinkin' he knows all about the weather and stuff. Besides, the bad stuff's not supposed to hit for another couple of hours. I say we go!" Then he hit his chest with both fists.

"You guys should come with," Matt said to Claudia, then turned to Arthur. "Bring fish boy with you. He'll be good for a laugh. Maybe we can feed him to the sharks."

Once again, Arthur felt the bile rising in his throat.

Where's a friendly octopus when you need it?

"Ah, thanks, but no thanks," Claudia replied. "I have better things to do than become a newspaper headline. And so should you. This is dumb."

"She's right," Arthur said in a clipped voice. "It's not safe."

"It's not safe? Listen to you! You sound like my mom!" Matt roared, and Arthur winced at the comment. "We'll get this thing in the water and see you losers later."

"Claudia, we can't just let them go—" Arthur protested.

"Do you think they're even listening?" Claudia shot back.

"See ya later, fish boy!" Matt yelled, as he and Mike pushed the catamaran into the turbulent ocean waves.

CHAPTER
SEVENTEEN

"LISTEN—NOW, LISTEN TO ME, everybody! This town is in danger! Now, several people have been killed already!"

Arthur scooped a handful of popcorn and shoved it toward his mouth. Some of the popcorn actually managed to go in, the rest falling on his lap.

Claudia made an "ewwwww" face. "Is that how your dad taught you to eat?" she said. "Gross."

"Shhhhhh!" Arthur said, his face glued to the TV screen. "This is the best part!"

"You've seen this movie a bazillion times!" Claudia replied.

"Thirty-one," Arthur corrected. "Well, thirty-two, now."

Arthur's dad had won the VCR in a holiday raffle at city hall a couple Christmases ago. Since then, Arthur had been taping his favorite movies whenever they would come on. About a year ago, he'd managed to record *The Blob*.

"What do you think's gonna happen to Matt and Mike and those guys?" Claudia asked as she took a bite of popcorn.

Arthur shrugged. "I dunno. Maybe the waves'll push 'em back to shore, and they'll just give up."

Claudia made a mock choking sound. "Yeah, Matt and Mike will definitely give up."

"Maybe not," Arthur said. "I just hope they don't get hurt."

Claudia nodded, and the two turned their attention back to the movie. An oozing creature had trapped a couple of teenagers and a small boy inside a diner and was threatening to overwhelm them. Arthur was on the edge of his seat, even after so many viewings.

"What, *The Blob* again?"

Arthur raised his head, and saw Tom standing in the kitchen doorway, wearing a raincoat.

"Dad," Arthur said. "You going out now?"

Tom buttoned the heavy raincoat. "Have to," he said. "Storm's coming in faster than expected. It's gonna be bad. Heard on the radio that we might even lose some fishing boats."

"Really?" Arthur said.

"Or worse," Tom said. "I'm headed out to the lighthouse. I'm just glad you two are safe inside. Stay put, now, y'hear?"

Arthur nodded sharply as Tom left the kitchen and opened the door. A gust of wind shot through the house.

"Arthur, you don't think . . . ," Claudia started to say. Then Arthur stood up without saying a word and hit the "pause" button on the VCR.

"Let's listen to the weather," he said and walked over to his dad's old AM/FM radio unit. He switched it on and dialed in the local news station.

"—gale-force winds already hitting the shores of Amnesty Bay. Storm surges are expected, with water reaching inland faster than anticipated."

"Storm surges?" Claudia said. "We learned about those in science class. The waves are gigantic."

Arthur walked away from the radio and looked outside the window. Rain was falling now, and the gray sky was rapidly changing to a dark gray, almost black on the horizon. The storm was rolling in now, full force. Trees were bending over, caught in the high winds that assaulted the shoreline. He looked up at the lighthouse and saw the rotating beacon in full operation.

"It's getting really bad out there," Arthur said.

"Authorities report that all fishing boats have returned to dock, but one boat seems to still be out in this inhospitable environment," the radio voice interrupted. "According to Amnesty Bay police, a catamaran was spotted heading out to sea roughly ninety minutes ago . . ."

Claudia gasped. "They're never gonna make it back in."

Arthur swallowed hard. "Not without some help."

CHAPTER
EIGHTEEN

"I WOULD JUST LIKE TO SAY FOR
the record that this is the worst idea in the
history of worst ideas!"

Claudia was standing on the shore,
screaming at Arthur, barely able to hold her
stance in the sand. The winds were punish-
ing, and it took all her effort to try to stay in
place. She shielded her eyes with her right
hand as the driving rain assaulted her from
the sky.

"If I don't go out there and get them,
they're gonna die!" Arthur yelled back. He

was walking forward somehow, pushing against the wind.

"Arthur, if you go out there, *you'll* die!" Claudia shouted. "And you're my friend! I don't want my friends to die! Then I have to make *new* friends! I *hate* making new friends!"

"Get into town!" Arthur yelled back, as the tide rolled in, shoving him backward. The storm was worsening, and water was coming into shore farther and farther with every swell. "Get the paramedics and the police and bring them here!"

"And just what are you going to do? Swim out there and drag them back?!" Claudia fumed.

"Something like that!" Arthur screamed, and he dived into the water headfirst.

And he didn't come up.

Claudia cursed under her breath, then ran back to the bike she had thrown onto the pavement. She jumped on and rode into town, the weather fighting her at every turn.

From the moment he hit the water, Arthur approached something like a state of shock. Not from the icy chill of the waters, nor from the extreme wind and rain, nor from the epic waves that were battering the shore. Instead, the shock came from how easy Arthur found it to swim in such conditions.

No, not just easy—like he was born to do it. He found himself swimming faster than he ever thought he could, somehow pulling ahead with every stroke despite the ocean's best efforts to thwart him. Not only was he pulling ahead, but he was speeding up.

He could see the catamaran now, just up ahead, but he was having difficulty keeping his head above water for more than a couple of seconds at a time. Whenever he popped his head out of the ocean, a wave came along and crashed into him, and the undertow dragged him back under. Then he would give a mighty kick, propelling

himself toward the surface, where he would bob up again.

Only this time, he didn't break the surface. He felt himself sucked down into the ocean, and no matter how hard he kicked, the water wouldn't let him go.

Arthur looked left, then right, and felt his heart beating. It felt like it was in his throat. Arthur didn't know how, but he could feel himself sweating an icy-cold sweat, even in the water. Every pore felt like it had opened up, and he was aware of his breathing.

My . . . breathing?

Blinking his eyes, Arthur realized that he actually was *breathing*.

Beneath. The. *Water*.

He gasped, taking in a lungful of salty liquid. Arthur expected to choke but was stunned to find that he simply sucked the water in and then out, just like breathing air. He didn't gag, he didn't feel like he was going to throw up, and his lungs didn't feel like they were going to collapse.

Somehow, Arthur was breathing underwater, just like in his dreams.

The panic subsided.

He felt the current tug at his legs, and just like that he was pulled downward, just like in his dreams.

Summoning his strength, Arthur gave a swift kick with his right leg, straight up. As he did, the world around him suddenly moved away. Arthur felt himself moving with a speed that he could only have imagined before. A second later, the dark water gave way to the surface as Arthur exploded outward.

What is going on?! Arthur thought, a good ten feet above the waves below. He saw Matt clinging to a life preserver, struggling against the waves, getting nowhere.

Arthur splashed back into the water, going down below the surface before coming back up again. With the slightest kick, he managed to stay afloat this time, half his torso above the rolling water line. The catamaran

was about twenty feet away from Matt. Arthur could make out Nikki and Mike at the catamaran's tiller, and Peanut, straining to hold on. The small boat was being tossed all around in the crashing waves, and the storm was only getting worse.

There's no way they're gonna make it.

Then he looked at Matt and saw him trying to hold on to the life preserver.

Just trying to hold on. And barely managing that.

"Matt!" Arthur screamed over the ocean's roar. "Hang on! I'm gonna come and get you!"

But how can I save him and save the kids on the boat? I can't do both. I need help! There's no way . . .

Arthur ducked beneath a wave and gave a kick. He propelled himself forward, only to hit the next wave beyond it. The water took Arthur with it, knocking him backward. He took a mouthful of water and spat it out instinctively, even as he realized he didn't need to anymore.

Need help . . .

The catamaran began to lean to the starboard side as the mast started to crack.

Then, just as Arthur had before, Matt started to bob beneath the surface. Even with the life preserver, the ocean and the storm were too formidable a foe.

Arthur kicked, swimming against the waves. He was making progress, but it was slow going. Too slow.

There was no way he could save everyone alone.

Then . . . he felt it.

Something swiped past his leg.

Then again.

And again.

Arthur dived below the water's surface, and saw a blank, featureless face staring back at him, its eyes wide, and determined. Then he saw the legs. Or rather, tentacles.

All eight of them.

Topo!

Can you help?

The octopus wrapped a tentacle around Arthur. He felt the limb tighten around his waist as Topo swam off, pulling Arthur along with him.

CHAPTER
NINETEEN

"PEANUT!"

Mike's voice rang out over the sound of the storm as he watched his friend washed overboard. He had lost his grip on the tiller. Mike had tried to grab Peanut, but the boat was tossing too hard, and Mike's skin was too wet and slick. His hand slipped, and Peanut hit the water, hard.

Again, Mike screamed for his friend who was no longer there. "Peanut!"

Then Mike screamed.

His jaw dropped when he saw Peanut

rise out from the ocean, a tentacle wrapped around his waist. Then, like a pitcher hurling a baseball, the tentacle flung Peanut toward the catamaran. The boy hit the portside hull, and Mike scrambled to his friend's side. Throwing his arms down, he grabbed onto Peanut and somehow managed to pull him back aboard.

"Was that a freakin' octopus?!" Mike stammered, white as a sheet. When he looked back at the ocean, he saw nothing except the waves.

And, peering out from them, a face he recognized instantly.

"Arthur?" Mike gasped in disbelief.

Bobbing up and down in the water, Arthur thrust his arms forward, heading for the boat. Then Topo broke the surface, the octopus's head right next to Arthur's. The two began to swim, and in mere moments, they reached Matt, who was losing his grip on the life preserver.

"How . . ." was all Matt managed to say as

he saw Arthur swimming to his side before he took in a mouthful of seawater and went under once more before bobbing up again.

"Don't talk!" Arthur yelled above the ocean.

And just as Matt was about to slip beneath the ocean's surface again, Arthur grabbed him.

He needs your help, Topo, Arthur thought. *You need to take him to the boat. Take him now!*

Arthur was still floored that the octopus could somehow understand his feelings, could react to them. As Arthur kept Matt's head above the water, Topo threw four tentacles around him—tight, but not too tight. Then the octopus started toward the catamaran.

The sky lit up as a bolt of lightning struck.

Thunder.

Rain.

Wind.

Arthur gaped as he saw the mast on the catamaran crack in two, falling into the ocean.

Buffeted by the gale-force winds, Arthur could only watch as the catamaran was tossed by the ocean's whims, hopelessly out of control.

CHAPTER TWENTY

THE OCTOPUS WAS USING ITS FREE tentacles to try to steady the catamaran, to keep it from capsizing, all while cradling Matt with its other limbs. Topo was doing its best to get Matt aboard the catamaran, but Arthur wondered if he would be any safer there than in the ocean.

The wind blew Arthur backward, and the waves crashed around him.

It's now or never, Arthur thought. *Either we bring everyone to shore now, or it ends here.*

Arthur swam over to Topo's side and looked at Matt, now unconscious. He checked to make sure Matt was breathing, which he was.

What else can you do? Arthur thought, looking at Topo. He could have sworn that the octopus was giving him a dirty look.

The storm was only getting worse. Moving quickly, Arthur swam up to the catamaran, and pulled himself up so he was half out of the water.

"Curry, what the hell?" Mike asked, as he held on to Peanut.

"How can you swim like that? How can you swim in this?" Nikki said, stunned at the sight.

"Give me that line," Arthur ordered, nodding his head sharply. Nikki grabbed the line from the broken mast and handed the end to Arthur.

"What are you gonna do?" Nikki yelled. "Are we gonna die?"

"No! Not today," Arthur said as he took

the line and dived back into the water. Then he shouted back to Mike, "Lock off the other end of the line on one of those boat hooks!"

"Lock off the other . . . ," Mike said with worry in his voice. "I . . . I don't know how to lock off anything! I don't know how to sail!"

"I do," Nikki said, and she took the other end of the line and began to wrap it around the boat hook, crisscrossing the line until it was tight. "All good!"

"Now hang on!" Arthur screamed, as he reared up. Before slipping below the surface, he saw that Topo had managed to put Matt safely aboard the catamaran.

Good, Arthur thought.

Beneath the water, Arthur took the other end of the line, and wrapped it around his waist. Then he tied a simple overhand knot to keep it in place. He hoped the knot would hold.

It would have to.

Now or never.

Arthur began kicking both legs, faster and

faster, and slowly he moved ahead, toward the shore.

Arthur was pulling the catamaran and amazed that he was doing so.

But his amazement turned to horror as he glanced back and saw the catamaran begin to sink.

CHAPTER
TWENTY-ONE

HE SCREAMED, BUT NOT OUT LOUD.

I need help! Someone to get this thing above water!

But there was no one around him. Just the kids on the catamaran, and they couldn't help themselves, let alone Arthur.

What am I gonna do?

For every stroke he took, the waves and the wind seemed to knock him back another ten feet. It was like a prizefight—the ocean itself was battling Arthur and determined to win.

The catamaran sank lower into the ocean, the kids scrambling to hang on.

Suddenly, the catamaran rose in the water. It wasn't sinking anymore, and Arthur couldn't understand why. He quickly ducked his head below the surface of the ocean, and then he saw them.

Dolphins.

Four of them, to be exact. They were swimming right beneath the catamaran, butting their heads up against the twin hulls, two dolphins to a hull.

Somehow, Arthur's desperate plea had been heard by unexpected saviors.

His courage redoubled, Arthur set to work.

The line tied around his waist, Arthur pulled and pulled, trying to bring the catamaran closer to shore. Every inch was pure agony. He felt like he was being torn in half, the sensation of pins and needles racing through his nerves. His muscles burned, like his body was on fire, despite the water all around him. The ocean just wouldn't stop fighting. Pulling and pushing and slamming and smashing. It refused to lose.

But so did Arthur.

He was moving against the current, somehow. It wasn't like that first time he kicked beneath the water, where he moved like a bullet toward the surface. It was slow going.

It was like slamming into a wall, over and over and over.

He felt battered, bruised.

Everything hurt.

And yet he kept fighting back.

Everything was white noise, his ears tortured by the water and wind. Arthur kept his head down, only looking up every now and then to make sure that he was still headed to shore. He had to constantly course-correct— the waves and current tried to put him off from his destination.

The ocean was vengeful today.

Not just the ocean was angry. The line tied around his waist was now cutting into it. Arthur could feel his skin, now raw, as

the rope rubbed against it. He was sure he was bleeding.

But still he strained, still he struggled, still he pulled.

Getting there, he thought. *Getting there. I am getting there, right?*

He felt light-headed. On the brink of exhaustion. Beyond the brink of exhaustion.

Head popping above the water, he saw the shore. Was he any closer? Or maybe he was farther out than he thought? He could no longer tell.

The light-headed feeling starting to over-take him as Arthur fell below the surface, still swimming, still kicking. The water seemed darker than it had before.

No, not the water.

Passing out.

He shook his head, trying not to succumb. As he swam, he darted in and out of dark-ness. He saw shapes forming before his eyes, even when he closed them.

The shapes swirled, and sparkled, and

Arthur tried not to see them, tried to look beyond, tried to keep swimming.

He took a breath and started to gag.

So tired . . .

The shapes continued to dance and bobble in the water all around Arthur. Then he saw something familiar.

Something . . . is . . . Topo?

No, not Topo. The octopus must still be back with the catamaran, doing its best to keep the boat steady.

It was something else. It was . . . a face . . .

I know that face, Arthur thought. *I know that face.*

He took another breath and didn't gag this time.

Then he kicked, *hard.*

Not today, he thought.

How long had he been swimming? Hours? Days? There was no sense of time, only the unending agony that filled every fiber of his body. And the undeniable determination to save them.

For Claudia.

He had to make it for Claudia.

For his dad.

For the kids.

He had to make it.

He thought his body was going to pull itself apart, and he wanted to stop—so many times he wanted to stop. To just let the ocean take him wherever it wanted.

But he couldn't.

He couldn't.

And then just as he felt himself slipping into blackness, he felt it. Beneath his feet. The smooth and tiny fragments between his toes. *Sand.*

Arthur stood up, saw the catamaran behind him, Topo using its tentacles to steady the boat. Arthur pulled until the boat was firmly on the shore, away from the ocean and the still-violent waves that washed to shore, as if trying to grab the boat once more. But it wasn't going to get that wish.

Not today.

The rain pounded him from above, and Arthur sank to his knees on the beach, his body spent.

Through the pouring rain, he made out the flashing lights from an ambulance and a police car. Arthur felt like he was having an out-of-body experience—as if his brain were a good ten feet above his body, and he was watching everything on the beach unfold before him, like he was watching it on TV.

He was light-headed and felt like he was going to pass out. Then he heard Claudia's voice. "You look terrible," she said, and he saw her drape a blanket around him, and she hugged him tightly.

"I do?" was all Arthur could manage before he collapsed on the sand. Claudia stayed with him until a paramedic ran over, and then he saw Claudia follow another paramedic to the catamaran. Together, they led the kids off the boat, and Claudia was there with an armful of blankets, giving them to Matt, Mike, Peanut, and Nikki.

He could hear Matt talking to Claudia. "Curry really did it," he said. "That kid . . . after all the stuff I said to him. He might be a freak, but he's a cool freak who saved us."

A police officer rushed over to Arthur, kneeling next to him. "You're Tom Curry's kid, aren't you?" he said.

Arthur nodded.

"You're a hero," the police officer said. "I don't know how you did it, but you did."

"I had . . . a little . . . help," Arthur said, before he finally did pass out.

CHAPTER
TWENTY-TWO

"I'M SORRY WE DON'T HAVE THE kind with the little marshmallows," Tom said. "I know you like that one."

Inside the Currys' kitchen, Arthur sat at the table, wrapped in a fluffy yellow blanket. He held a mugful of hot chocolate tightly in both hands. He stuck his mouth and nose into the mug, inhaling deeply, feeling the warmth flood his nostrils.

"S'okay," Arthur said, taking a slow sip. The liquid burned his mouth and throat, but it felt good.

I'm surprised I can feel anything, he thought.

He took another drink of hot chocolate, then set the mug on the table.

I think my arms are gonna fall off.

"Do you wanna do this now, or do you wanna wait?" Tom asked.

"We can do it now," Arthur said. "I have it coming."

"You certainly do. This is the part where I tell you just how incredibly stupid that was, going out into the ocean all alone," Tom said.

"But—" Arthur protested.

"Nuh-uh," Tom stopped him. "Not done yet. What I should do, is ground you for the rest of the summer. Maybe the rest of the year."

"But—" Arthur tried to interject.

"But I'm not going to, because I am so, so proud of you. So unbelievably proud of you."

"You are?"

"Of course I am! You risked everything for those kids, Arthur. You didn't even think about yourself. That's something . . . ," Tom

said, struggling to find the right words. "That's something your mom would have done."

Tom sat down at the table, grabbed his son's hands, and looked right into his eyes.

"I can't lose you, Arthur. I promised your mother I would take care of you. And I thought for a minute there, when the police called me and told me what you'd done, I thought . . ."

Arthur didn't say anything. He just kept looking at his father.

He heard the sound of the storm outside, the rain hitting the aluminum siding. Wind rattled the windows.

"What you did out there . . ."

"I didn't know I could swim like that," Arthur said. "I don't know how I did that. Any of it. I don't . . . How did I get so strong? So fast? I've never felt like that before."

"You take after her, you know," Tom said. "Headstrong. Stubborn. Strong. She would be proud."

"Do you think so?" Arthur asked.

"I know so," Tom replied. He stood up from the table and walked toward the door. Just as he was leaving, Tom turned around. "You know you are grounded for the rest of the week, though, right?"

Arthur smiled. "Yeah. I know."

CHAPTER
TWENTY-THREE

"I THOUGHT YOU WERE GROUNDED for the rest of eternity."

Arthur turned from his perch on the rock, looking at the sandy beach behind him. There was Claudia, walking toward him, her bike resting on the ground. He smiled at her, then looked back at the ocean. Topo was by his side, and Arthur was resting one hand on Topo's head.

"I don't think my dad had the heart to follow through," Arthur said. "I think he

thinks I've been through enough, and that I've learned my lesson."

Claudia climbed up the rock and sat down next to Arthur. "And have you?"

"Have I what?"

Claudia laughed. "Have you learned your lesson?"

Arthur smiled and looked at the ocean. It was much calmer now. The storm had passed a few days before. Strands of seaweed dotted the shore, kicked up by the violent ocean currents. He felt a tentacle tap his hand, and he watched as Topo waved with another tentacle and slid back into the water.

"See ya later, Topo," Arthur said.

"That's gonna take some getting used to," Claudia said, shaking her head. "So, did you?"

"My lesson?" Arthur pondered. "I have no idea. I mean, going after the boat was dumb. So, so dumb. But . . . if I hadn't, I would never have learned what I can do."

"So," Claudia said, her voice growing softer, "what you told me about your mom . . . it was all true?"

EPILOGUE

HE WATCHED THE OCTOPUS WAVE,
and a moment later, it disappeared beneath
the surface of the water.

"It's always good to see you, old friend,"
Arthur said out loud. He tugged at his beard
and smiled at the ocean.

"It's always good to see you, too," a voice
said from behind.

Arthur turned around and saw Tom Curry.
His father.

They threw their arms around each other
and embraced like only a father and son could.

"It's good to be home," Arthur said.